DEATH
UNDER THE
PERSEIDS

Also by Teresa Dovalpage

Death Comes in through the Kitchen

Queen of Bones

Death of a Telenovela Star

DEATH UNDER THE PERSEIDS

Teresa Dovalpage

Published by Soho Press, Inc.
227 W 17th Street
New York, NY 10011

This is a work of fiction. Names, characters, places, and incidents either are the product of the author's imagination or are used fictitiously, and any resemblance to actual persons, living or dead, businesses, companies, events, or locales is entirely coincidental.

Library of Congress Cataloging-in-Publication Data

Names: Dovalpage, Teresa, author.
Title: Death under the perseids / Teresa Dovalpage.
Description: New York, NY : Soho Crime, [2021]
Identifiers: LCCN 2021027168

ISBN 978-1-64129-216-0
eISBN 978-1-64129-217-7

Subjects: GSAFD: Mystery fiction.
Classification: LCC PS3604.O936 D47 2021
DDC 813'.6—dc23
LC record available at https://lccn.loc.gov/2021027168

Interior design by Janine Agro

Printed in the United States of America

10 9 8 7 6 5 4 3 2 1

The Tears of St. Lorenzo

Las lágrimas de San Lorenzo, that's what we call them in Spanish. In English, it's the Perseid meteor shower. I prefer "the tears of Saint Lawrence," though they remind me of those I shed for *my* Lorenzo, who died roasted like his namesake.

Do you know the story of Saint Lawrence the martyr? He was a Roman deacon condemned to being burned alive in a gridiron. In the middle of his torment, he said to the executioner, "I'm well done on this side. You can turn me over now."

What did Lorenzo say while he was being cooked? Did he suffer? Did he ever forgive me?

PART I:
Waiting in Port

1: Surprise Tickets

The cruise ship *Narwhal*, all twelve decks of her, towered above the terminal building. It had a festive air, with the hull painted white and bright ribbons of red, yellow and green splashed all over. From a distance it looked like a giant tropical bird that had inexplicably landed on water.

August in Miami was, as usual, ninety-four degrees with a devilish mix of heat and humidity that made you want to crawl inside a refrigerator. The Nautilus instructions said to be at Terminal B before noon, but it was well past one and the line to enter the building wasn't moving. It was worse than being at an airport, *por Dios!* Then I remembered that we had no right to complain. After all, we had gotten the cruise for free.

I WAS STILL SCRATCHING my head about the whole thing. It all began when a young woman showed up at Pretty and Pampered, the pet grooming salon where

I worked part-time, asking for me. She looked like a teenager, but dressed professionally in a beige suit, and introduced herself as a Nautilus representative. I was getting ready to give a summer cut to a standard poodle when she presented me with an embossed envelope and cooed, "Congratulations, Ms. Spivey! You've just won two cruise tickets to Havana!"

I was born and raised in Havana. After marrying Nolan in 2008, I had returned many times to visit my grandmother but never thought of taking a *cruise* back. And in July 2017, sailing to Cuba was the last thing on my mind. "I've won what?" I asked.

The poodle took advantage of my surprise to get away and hide under a chair.

"A couple of tickets!" the girl chirped, perky as could be. "Aboard the *Narwhal*, our most popular ship! The cruise's departing on August the tenth."

Nautilus Cruise Line had started to offer short cruises that included Cuba in their itineraries, she explained. They were carrying out their biggest ever promotional campaign with many giveaways. I was one of the lucky winners. Cool, eh? What that chick didn't say was how and where I had signed up for the raffle or whatever it was that I had won.

I used to enter sweepstakes that promised everything

from five hundred dollars a week for life to a grand prize of a million, or a Porsche, or a weekend in Paris, but that was a long time ago. It had finally dawned on me that most were a waste of time, if not outright scams. I didn't know how these Nautilus people found me either, but I guess everybody's information is online nowadays. Besides, the idea of winning something, anything, was appealing. I kept my mouth shut and accepted the "gift."

As soon as the girl left, Candela hugged me. She smelled of patchouli, sandalwood incense and, faintly, wet dog hair.

"I'm so happy for you!" she said. "That's the start of the hot streak I told you about. *¿Viste?*"

I didn't "see" anything clearly, but went along with her.

Candela and I had met at a Starbucks in 2011. Nolan and I had been in Gainesville for around five months, and I already missed Miami and the friends I made there. Not that there were many. Since I didn't drive yet, I couldn't go out on my own to meet new people, and my husband's colleagues wouldn't have anything to do with me. I needed someone to talk to. To vent, actually. In my own language.

So I was waiting for my iced caramel macchiato

when someone said *coño* aloud. *Coño* is like the Free-masons' secret handshake for Cubans. I looked up and saw a young woman, curvy and petite, with arms covered in jingling silver bracelets and a zodiac sign necklace.

"You Cuban?" I asked shyly in English.

"Kind of." She smiled. "*You* are."

Daughter and granddaughter of Cubans, Candela spoke fluent, if at times old-fashioned, Spanish. She was into esoteric stuff—astrology, the Law of Attraction, the Ascended Masters, the whole metaphysical enchilada. She said she liked my aura that first day. I just liked hanging out with someone who cursed in public. We became fast friends.

When she opened Pretty and Pampered, I joined her as a "pet stylist." I didn't know much about styling pets but enjoyed working with cats and dogs, and even the occasional rabbit—why anybody would want to groom a *rabbit* is beyond my understanding. The *cochinos* stink and bite, and I got three stitches after a Holland Lop tried to take off my finger.

The weekend before the ticket surprise, Candela had read the Tarot for me. I got the upright Wheel of Fortune, one of the most auspicious cards for money, according to her, and the Eight of Wands, up too, indicating a trip. I also drew the Star Reversed. "A warning sign, but you got two good cards out of three," she concluded. "The Star Reversed just means you should be careful, now that so many wonderful things are bound to happen."

Even if I didn't believe in Tarot, the Eight of Wands card popped into my head when I opened the envelope with the Nautilus Cruise Line logo.

I thought of Nolan too. His job situation had him all stressed out. The cruise could be turned into something fun, a second honeymoon of sorts. We hadn't had much intimacy, sexual or otherwise, for months. I hadn't called him "*papito*," my romantic nickname for him, in a long time. He needed a vacation, poor guy. So did I.

Candela passed me the poodle, who wasn't happy to be back on the grooming table.

"You're going to live *la vida loca* for a few days, Merceditas. It'll do you good!"

Candela was the only person in Gainesville who called me Merceditas—the affectionate form of Mercedes. Everybody else called me Mercy; Merceditas was too long and difficult to pronounce for most Americans, including my husband. I had tried using Mercedes, but people kept asking why I had been named after a car.

I reread the letter. Though it seemed legit, that was the first time I had heard of the company. I knew Carnival—Nolan and I had taken one of their *el cheapo* Cancún cruises when we lived in Miami. Viking and Princess were familiar names from the ads. But Nautilus?

Candela said it was a small but well-established company that catered to "older people with disposable income." Seeing that I didn't fit into that category, I asked her to call their main office—my accent is a problem over the phone because I tend to drop the final consonants. They confirmed that there was a paid-for reservation in my name, a balcony stateroom for two.

"It's all good, *chica!*" she said, her silver charms tinkling as she spun around. "*Estate tranquila* and don't be so suspicious of everything. You have to start trusting the universe. Now let's go celebrate!"

And so we did at La Margarita Bar and Grill. Nolan had a fit when I came home around midnight, tired and tipsy. But when I told him about the cruise the next morning, he got over it fast.

"It's a godsend, Mercy," he said. "Just what we need."

In truth, *he* needed it more than I did. It had been a strange and difficult year for him.

The rough spell started in March when his daughter, Katy, who had moved to Albuquerque, disinvited him from her wedding, asking her maternal uncle to walk her down the aisle instead. She'd become incensed when Nolan wanted to include me in the invitation, though I had no desire whatsoever to be part of it. Katy had once been his favorite, and they had been close until he divorced her mother to marry "the Cuban homewrecker."

A few weeks later, a certain Doctor Fernández, a Cuban professor, asked Nolan to give a lecture at the University of Havana in the late summer. The catch was, he discovered later, that Doctor Fernández couldn't buy him a plane ticket "because of the embargo." That was a lie the size of the *Narwhal*. He simply expected Nolan to pay for his own airfare and stay. That's how things work in Cuba: you're a foreigner, you pay for everything.

Nolan had accepted and was looking forward to the trip—it was an honor, he assured me, to be invited by my (almost) alma mater. But then, in May, he lost his job. Though Point South College didn't actually fire him, they didn't renew his contract, which was the same for all practical purposes. He didn't have tenure, so there was nothing he could do.

His firing didn't surprise me. Nolan was very liberal. Point South was a small private college with conservative views. He'd had disagreements with both his department chair and his dean several times over the years, and they finally decided to get rid of him. There had been warning signs, subtle and not so much, like the day he came home stunned because no one had asked him to be part of the hiring committee for a new literature professor. (Later he figured out that they were interviewing his replacement.) Or when they sent everybody in his department, except him, to a professional development conference in Las Vegas. He knew that his Point South days were numbered.

In truth, he had never liked his stuffy colleagues or the college's conservative bent. He still pined for the status and privilege he had once enjoyed as a tenured and popular professor at Florida International University—until I showed up and turned his life upside down.

In any case, after he was let go, he panicked. He had made some inquiries and sent his resume to a few colleges in a frenzied flurry, but none had been answered yet. He talked about teaching Spanish at a local high school, but that wasn't going to work either. I knew, because I had been an occasional sub, how sassy and plain disrespectful those kids were. They would eat him alive.

Suddenly, spending several hundred dollars on a trip to Havana to deliver an unpaid lecture didn't sound like a good idea. He was ready to turn down the invitation, but the free cruise changed his mind. That, and the fact that the gig would fluff up his résumé. He was planning to attend the Modern Language Association's annual convention in January to meet with future employers. In my non-scholarly eyes, the convention was a huge boring meeting where jaded or out-of-work professors and hopeful graduate students listened to dull presentations and nosed around for jobs.

NOT EVEN A HINT of a breeze blew in from the nearby ocean. Nolan's shoulders were slumped. His eyes were glassy. He must have been worn out after driving non-stop all the way from Gainesville. I was hot and hungry. But we were hopeful, fully expecting that the cruise would signal a reversal of fortune. It was long overdue.

2: The Man of My Life

On days like this, when Nolan hadn't had a good night's sleep, he showed his age. He was nineteen years my senior. People who met us for the first time frequently assumed he was my father, which never failed to annoy him. I didn't mind the assumptions— they were nothing new for me. I always fell for older guys.

Like Lorenzo. He was thirty-five when we met. I was eighteen, a junior at the Faculty of Arts and Letters. My major was art history, not because I had any interest in art or history, but because my best friend, Julia, had convinced me that the classes were easy and fun. They weren't. Two-hour visits to Old Havana led by Eusebio Leal, the city historian, to admire porticos and columns left me with a migraine. I couldn't tell the baroque from the Romantic periods, or the classical from the postclassical. Flunking was in the cards, as Candela would have put it.

The only course I liked was a contemporary Cuban literature class. The professor, Lorenzo Alvear, had beautiful handwriting, full of curlicues. That was the second thing I noticed about him—the first was his biceps. He was tall and dark-haired, with big caramel eyes. He wore his hair longer than most guys did in our straitlaced college environment. Sometimes he even tied it in a ponytail, which was pushing it. Male students and professors were advised, often strongly, to keep their hair military short. But Lorenzo was also a writer, and that gave him special privileges. His short stories had been published in Cuban magazines like *Bohemia* and *El Caimán Barbudo*.

I turned up the charm, used all my *mañas y marañas*, and he couldn't resist. Not to brag, but few guys could, back then. By the end of the semester—after our first date at the National Library—the cool professor and I were a couple. Though Lorenzo had preferred not to "publicize" it, I had told Julia and she likely spread the word, at least among the students. Not that anyone cared. Girls who had flirted in vain with him were jealous, but even they admitted that, like Macarena in the catchy Los del Rio song, I had a body that deserved *alegría y cosa buena*. I wore my blond hair long and wasn't shy to flaunt my toned legs and generous derriere. As for Lorenzo, he brought me happiness and good things.

Though I wasn't an intellectual like him, not even a good student, we had clicked in every possible way. In bed, and *that's* important, but we also talked a lot. About life, death and everything in between. Despite the age difference, we were a good match. We had fun together. I'm sure he'd had affairs with other students before, and maybe a few colleagues as well. But once our relationship became serious, he wouldn't so much as look at anybody else. He valued loyalty. That was why he was so furious when . . .

Poor Lorenzo. I felt guilty for a long time, but what happened to him wasn't my fault. I was already out of the country when he did what he did. What people *said* he did. Nobody knew back then whether it had been an accident or suicide.

An image that had haunted me since I'd first heard the story—his body charred beyond recognition—replaced the happy sight of the cruise ship. Despite my efforts to keep the past at bay, it returned in full force. Not that my efforts had ever paid off. No matter how many years had passed since we had seen each other for the last time, I still thought of him. More often than I wanted to admit, even to myself.

The truth was, I had never forgotten him.

Lorenzo hadn't had an easy life. When he was a teenager, his father, a stonemason, fell from a scaffold and died on the spot. His mother then spiraled into depression. A year later, she started having renal problems and had to go on dialysis, which she hated. "Your weakest organ fails when you're heartsick," Lorenzo once told me. "Mom had inherited bad kidneys, but it wasn't until she stopped caring about life that sickness claimed her."

One day he came home to find his mother gone and the entire building smelling like burned flesh. She had set herself on fire, her last act etched forever on the darkened ceilings and smoke-stained walls. Lorenzo spent the remainder of his last high school year with a crazy aunt. Afterward, he was pretty much on his own.

In the meantime, his next-door neighbor, a woman named Bárbara, had taken over Lorenzo's space—the two families shared what had originally been one large apartment on top of a grocery store. She refused to let Lorenzo in, but the authorities intervened on his behalf and forced her to retreat to her part of the building. Afterward, Bárbara and Lorenzo patched things up, but he never totally trusted her again. During her brief stay in his "apartment," she had stolen everything he owned, he said, except for his books.

And yet, despite his losses, Lorenzo wasn't a sad man. A little melancholic, yes. But by the time we met, he was one of the most eligible bachelors at the University of Havana, or at least at the Faculty of Arts and Letters, where he had been hired right after finishing his master's degree. He had restored the apartment, painting the ceiling light blue and the walls white. He kept publishing short stories and later found a literary agent who agreed to represent *Las Perseidas*, a novel that had taken him five years to write.

The book turned out to be the cause of his downfall and, some said, even his death. An envious colleague accused him of writing a counterrevolutionary novel and working with "*agentes del enemigo*." (It seemed like the colleague didn't know the difference between a literary agent and a spy.) The allegations were unfounded, but Lorenzo spent several weeks in prison and lost his job.

Though I had already broken up with him, the political police called me in for questioning. I explained that Lorenzo's book was about aliens, spacecrafts and the Perseid meteor shower, not politics. His foreign friends were liberal intellectuals who either sympathized with the revolution, like Nolan, or at least didn't criticize it, like The Viking. It all had been a huge misunderstanding, but by the time the truth came out, it was too late . . .

Lorenzo and I spent less than two years together, but maybe we were destined to be married. Maybe we were soulmates or something of that sort. And I blew it big time. Because even after so much time had passed, even after the guy was, you know, *dead*, saying his name aloud made the hair on the back of my neck stand up.

Nolan suspected it. I had opened my big mouth and said a few things that should have gone unmentioned. Like when I had made a stupid comment, something to the effect that my last boyfriend always gave me gardenias, and what was *his* flower going to be? Petunias? It was silly, but Nolan had taken it the wrong way and barked that he would rather not be privy to details of my former love life.

Candela was my only friend in Gainesville who knew about Lorenzo. One evening, over dirty mojitos at La Margarita Bar and Grill, I admitted that he had been "*el hombre de mi vida.*" She immediately dragged me to a séance to contact his spirit and ask if "the man of my life" still loved me. The psychic medium wasn't having a good day, though, because she couldn't make the astral connection. Candela had been left disappointed. So had I.

NOLAN WAS BUSY WITH his phone, texting or emailing. I turned to another guy in line and said, "Can't wait to see what the cabins look like."

"Sometimes they aren't ready until a couple hours after we get on board," he answered. "But that's okay because the bars are open. That's what counts, don't you think?"

"You bet!"

Nolan put the phone away and scowled at the mention of bars. He thought I drank too much. I disagreed. Occasionally I had one too many margaritas with Candela, but not every day, not even every week. Drinking was just a way of having fun, not dealing with problems—as I had done the first time I got *borracha*, after my embarrassing fling with Kiel.

3: The Viking

The memory of The Viking made my skin crawl. I shouldn't have slept with him—or attempted to. Kiel Ostargó—the Cuban pronunciation of his first and last names—was a shy, stolid Dane who had been friends with Lorenzo for ages, way before I entered their lives.

They had met in the late nineties, when Lorenzo, still a graduate student at the University of Havana, was invited to the Centre Pompidou in Paris for a literature conference that Kiel had also attended. They hit it off after discovering they read the same books and—it seemed to me—enjoyed discussing obscure authors and novels nobody else knew or cared to know. But to each their own.

Kiel had a degree in Latin American literature. He spoke Spanish, English and French, besides his native language. But he didn't need to put his skills to use teaching or translating. His parents had moved to the

United States when he was very young. They rented a house in Chicago. (Or was it Boston? When I first heard the story, all these American cities sounded the same to me: faraway places I couldn't find on a map.) There was an explosion in their home. His parents died; he survived but was badly burned. He had scars on his torso, face and hands, and his hair stopped growing. I never saw him without a shaggy blond wig, even when we . . .

He'd also ended up with some sort of brain damage that forced him to write everything down. He would forget his hotel address, his email passwords, even his own phone number. Lorenzo, who had a photographic memory, taught him some tricks to retain information, but I don't think they helped much. He often stopped midphrase, as if waiting for the right word. Though of course, he was communicating in his third or fourth language.

As the only survivor, Kiel got a compensation settlement, a seven-digit amount that he used to go to college and later travel the world. After their meeting in Paris, Lorenzo invited him for Christmas, and Havana soon became his favorite destination. People were so nice! The weather was so perfect! "You Cubans," he said once, "are the warmest, kindest human beings on the planet."

It didn't hurt that he possessed what—to our

third-world eyes—amounted to unlimited funds, concluded the cynic in me. He always struck me as a little naïve. My female friends kept asking to be introduced to the "rich guy who talked funny," but Lorenzo didn't let anyone take advantage of Kiel. "He can find his own girlfriends when he wants to."

For most of the time I knew him, he showed no interest in girls and was shy around them, even me. His scars probably made him self-conscious, but he enjoyed life in other ways. Every summer he went fishing to Jardines de la Reina, a secluded marine park, with a Revolutionary Armed Forces general. Kiel talked affectionately of the "great old warrior" who had nicknamed him The Viking. He had brought a Segway for the general's son and a *quinceañera* dress for his daughter. He'd also financed Lorenzo's subscriptions to literary journals and even trips to Modern Language Association's conferences.

Nothing odd about it. Lorenzo was so easygoing and sociable that even perfect strangers were inclined to help him. But Kiel was no stranger. Which made my actions even more unforgivable.

THE LINE STARTED TO move, and we finally made it into the air-conditioned terminal building. I went to the restroom, refreshed my makeup and texted Candela: ALMOST THERE!

She texted back: HAVE FUN. HOW'S EL COMEMIERDA DOING?

I answered with a thinking emoji.

Candela called Nolan a shiteater, a *mosca muerta* (which means a dead fly, but also a two-faced person) and worse. He returned the favor, saying that she was silly and woo-woo with her Tarot cards, sandalwood lotions and zodiac jewelry. If Candela and I had experienced friendship at first sight, there had been instant enmity between her and Nolan. Though he never said it, I knew that he was jealous of all the time I spent with her. He also thought that we spoke Spanish too fast for him to understand. Not that we did it on purpose—it was just the Cuban way.

I returned to the line and kissed him on the cheek. He smiled but didn't kiss me back. A look of concern was still plastered over his face, his beady blue eyes windows of hopelessness.

My poor *comemierda* wasn't doing too well.

I took out the schedule that Nautilus had sent us in advance. We would have a day and a half in Havana and two in Nassau. Nolan's lecture was arranged for our only full day in Havana, which I planned to spend with Mamina—my paternal grandmother, though she'd raised me as if I were her daughter.

"Passengers with foreign passports, please move to this side," an officer said. "If you were born in Cuba, even if you're a naturalized American, get in this line too."

There had been an outcry in 2016 when the Ministry of Tourism announced that Cuban-born passengers weren't allowed back by ship. By airplane, yes. Cruise, no. What kind of rule was that? US-based Cubans threatened to sue cruise lines for discrimination, even those who had no intention to go back, on a cruise or otherwise. In the end, the head honchos convinced Raúl Castro, or whoever was in charge, to let everyone in by all modes of transportation. The only requirement was that we had to show our Cuban passport, no matter if we were American citizens now.

Nolan had no such problems. He had only needed his American passport and a tourist visa that a Nautilus representative helped him get through their people-to-people program.

With my two passports in hand, I moved to the second queue, behind a white-haired, wiry guy in a Grateful Dead T-shirt with a swath of gold chains around his neck. Classy. I caught him ogling me, and I gave him the evil eye.

4: The Writer Who Taught

I distracted myself by guessing, based on their accents, where the passengers in my line had come from. There were two Mexican families and an Argentinian-sounding couple. The others could be Europeans or Canadians. I thought that I was likely to be the only Cuban. We didn't need to "discover" the country or pay thousands of dollars to have a people-to-people experience—we already had enough of that aboard the crowded buses we called "camels."

As if to prove me wrong, the woman behind me touched my elbow and asked in Cuban-accented Spanish, "Am I supposed to show them my green card?"

She wore a blue polyester dress that clashed with an oversized red fake leather purse. Nobody has ever accused my countrymen and women of having any fashion sense. But some of us (ahem!) learn. I was wearing a white cotton dress with brown espadrilles and a *real* leather purse.

"They only want to look at passports now," I said. "You'll need your green card to reenter the United States, though."

"Thank you, *niña*."

I was too old to be called "girl," but that's a Cuban for you. The woman touched my arm again as if she had known me forever.

"Aren't you Merceditas Montero?"

Montero was my maiden name, which I hadn't used in years.

"Yes," I answered, surprised. "Have we met before?"

"Don't you remember me? I was your professor at the Faculty of Arts and Letters."

She looked like Selfa Segarra, the woman who had supposedly turned Lorenzo in to the Seguridad. Who still lived in Cuba, for all I knew. I did a double take, but no doubt it was her.

Back in the day, when I was in college, Selfa and Lorenzo had been not only colleagues but friends. At least, Lorenzo thought they were. He let her read a copy of *Las Perseidas* and people said she had reported him and his "subversive book" to the political police.

I stared hard at her. Her hair, which she used to wear short and light brown, was dirty-gray and uncut. You could serve soup in her marionette lines and the deep wrinkles on her forehead. She had gained weight and grown a double chin. Her dress didn't do her figure (to the extent she had one) any favors. Her collection of plastic bracelets came from Ñooo ¡que barato!, Miami's cheapest discount store. I noticed all this in the few seconds that lapsed between her question and the insincere smile that accompanied my answer.

"Ah, Professor Segarra. Yes, I remember you."

"Please, call me Selfa."

I nodded dismissively. She started gabbing, saying she'd moved to Miami two years ago to take care of her grandson but didn't like it there.

"I've tried to find a job at a community college, but nobody wants me. After heading the Literature Department at the Faculty of Arts and Letters, I'm now working in a nursing home. As a health aide, imagine that!"

It made me happy to hear that she had ended up wiping old people's *culos*. That is, until I remembered that I had been cleaning other people's *dogs'* asses recently.

"My son died in 2015," she went on. "He was just twenty-eight. My daughter-in-law works all day and has no relatives here. That's why she sent for me."

Her son, who sang in an amateur rock band in Havana,

would show up on campus on a beat-up motorcycle and wearing, to Selfa's embarrassment, an Aerosmith T-shirt. Unlike his mother, an active Communist Party member, he was a fan of all things American.

"I'm sorry, Selfa. What happened to him?"

"He was found dead on Miami Beach with a needle stuck in his left arm. Overdose, the cops concluded, but my Vladimir wasn't a drug addict. He had a job at Publix and was doing so well."

What was a mother going to say? I listened respectfully.

"Besides, he was left-handed." Her eyes swelled with tears. "Even if—he wouldn't have held the syringe with his right hand. Someone did that to him. But the police didn't care to find out."

"That's terrible."

Worse than what she had done to Lorenzo, I added to myself. Her mouth quivered when she spoke again.

"What about you? How did you get here?"

"I married an American man."

I didn't go into specifics, not wanting the chat with Selfa to stretch out for longer than necessary. And yet, despite my obvious lack of interest, she continued to chew my ear off about her grandkid, her poorly paid job and how much she missed Havana.

At first, it puzzled me why she acted so friendly toward the former girlfriend of the man she'd sent to prison—supposing the rumors were true. But as she rattled on, I realized she didn't know that Lorenzo and I had been a couple. Odd, considering how nosy she was, but we had always been careful around his colleagues.

Selfa's prattle started getting on my nerves. I was ready to pull out my cellphone and pretend to take a call when she said something that caught my attention.

". . . much less money for traveling, but it would have been crazy to turn down a free trip."

"What do you mean, a free trip?"

"A woman came to the nursing home and told me I had won a cruise. I didn't even know the company, but wasn't about to argue with her. Especially after she handed me a ticket with my name on it."

Sweat began trickling down my temples despite the air conditioning.

"I've gone back to Cuba only once." Selfa lowered her voice. "As a mule, because I can't afford to go any other way. I thought it'd be nice to be on a cruise, but I'm scared to death."

I was getting scared too.

"That woman who went looking for you, what did she look like?"

"A pretty girl. Very young."

"How did she find you? If you hadn't entered any sweepstakes—" *That* was what had been bothering me about my own ticket as well.

"Oh, but I probably did! I must have written the address, or at least the name of the nursing home, somewhere." She fumbled with the buttons of her dress. Her nails were short and bitten. "I didn't want to probe, in case it was a mistake," she added. "This is the first time in my life that I've won anything."

"Funny that you and I happened to win the same raffle, or whatever it was," I said slowly. "By the way, this is the first time that *I've* won anything either."

Her eyes widened.

"Did you also—?"

"Yup."

There was an uncomfortable pause, with silence as a toothless grin exchanged between us. Then we both smiled. A forced, constipated smile.

"A pair of lucky Cubans," she said flatly.

How many free cruises had Nautilus given away—to people who didn't even remember signing up for the deal?

"What are you scared of?" I asked.

Her lips trembled.

"I don't know. The ship sinking—"

"The *Narwhal* looks pretty unsinkable. See how big she is?"

"So was the *Titanic*."

"Ah, come on, Selfa."

"I've been having nightmares for weeks about the deep sea. Tropical storms, monster waves—almost canceled the trip." She sighed. "I could have used the money, but my ticket was nonrefundable. And I still have this gut feeling . . . Honestly, before I saw you, I was ready to turn around and just go home."

I felt sorry for her and patted her arm reassuringly. After all, she was an old woman who had suffered a big loss.

"Everything will be fine, Selfa. This isn't stormy season. My husband and I went on another Caribbean cruise around this time and didn't see any big waves. There are so many fun things to do on board, you'll forget you're at sea."

"That's good to know. Thank you, *mija*. I wish my daughter-in-law and my grandson could have come with me, but it was way too expensive."

"You only got one ticket?"

"Yes. Did you get two?" I nodded, and she made a visible effort to look happy for me. "That's amazing! I hope you and your husband have a great time."

Her manners had softened with age. She wasn't just older, but humbler and more vulnerable, so different from the snobbish professor she used to be. She had a doctorate in literature and had looked down on Lorenzo and others who only had their master's degrees. But she didn't prepare for her classes; even mediocre students like me noticed she didn't know what she was talking about half the time.

Selfa didn't care. She liked to introduce herself as "a writer who taught" and had been attempting for years to peddle *Profesora Día y Noche*, a novel based on her own life, when *Las Perseidas* became a finalist for the Saint Jordi award. She couldn't stand the idea that Lorenzo's book was on its way to be published in Spain when even Cuban editors weren't interested in hers.

If she had in fact turned him in to the political police, she had been harshly punished, perhaps by fate or karma. Candela was always talking about karmic retribution, but the notion never really rang true to me. Life wasn't fair most of the time. Period. Only occasionally a glimpse of justice surfaced. In Selfa's case, the punishment seemed excessive. Misplaced too. Her wrongs weren't her son's fault.

The guy with the gold chains went through the checkpoint. I was next.

"See you around, Selfa."

"Yes! Let's find each other later, Merceditas. I hate being on my own."

My documents were inspected quickly and my Cuban passport stamped. When I walked away with a goodbye wave, Selfa was nervously searching her purse, as if she had forgotten something.

"Anyone else with foreign passports?" the checkpoint screener asked.

Two men approached the counter. One was a skinny, gray-bearded guy in a tie-dyed shirt who looked like a hippie—or at least my idea of what a hippie was. He went first. The other, who walked with a slight limp, carried a burgundy European Union passport. Our eyes met for a second, and I couldn't shake the feeling that I had seen him before. Maybe the other guy too. They both seemed sort of familiar. My throat closed and my heart pounded faster.

I attempted to reason with my absurdly frightened self. Yes, it had been a disagreeable surprise to meet Selfa here, but Nautilus could have given away dozens of tickets. After all, they were looking to compete with Carnival, the biggest cruise line in the world. They needed to get their name out there, and freebies helped. As for the two guys, probably just a passing resemblance to people I'd met before.

Everything will be fine.

I moved to another counter, where my picture was taken and inserted into an ID card. The card would be used for onboard purchases and scanned when I got off and back on the ship, the clerk explained. It would also be my room key. Talk about multitasking!

I got out of the way of the crowd to wait for Nolan. The American line was dwindling. After his documents were finally checked and he was issued his own card, we walked through a metal detector like the ones they used at the airport. Their presence, usually an annoyance, was comforting this time. At least no one could get on the ship with a gun or a knife. But who would want to? And why?

5: Merceditas

Candela was right. I needed to be more *tranquila*, to chill out and start "trusting the universe," whatever that meant. But I had always been suspicious of everybody and everything. The only person I ever trusted completely from the beginning (besides Mamina, of course) was Lorenzo. I understood him and his issues because I had my own as well.

For starters, I'd grown up without parents. And the way my mother vanished from my life was bad enough to traumatize anyone. She was a young American who had traveled to Cuba in the eighties and fallen in love with my dad. They got married, and I was born in 1987. Three years later, she up and left without warning. Just like that. I never heard from her again. No letters, no phone calls. Nada. My father died in Angola in 1991, so I ended up an orphan, like Lorenzo. Thank God for Mamina, who came from her Pinar del Río ranch to raise me. She was the only mother I ever knew.

My birth mother's name was Tania Rojas—which sounded like an alias if she was really American. But she hadn't left behind any documents that could identify her, not even a picture. When I asked what she looked like, Mamina directed me to the closest mirror. She said I had inherited my mother's blue eyes, long limbs and freckled nose, features that made me look "exotic" in Cuba and helped me blend here. Fortunately, a larger-than-average *culo* was also passed down from my paternal ancestors.

Candela, who liked to play shrink, maintained that I had married Nolan because I subconsciously wanted to come to the United States and look for my birth mother. She suggested I contact her cousin Marlene Martínez, who used to be a cop in Cuba, to help me find my runaway mom. Marlene owned a bakery in Miami, La Bakería Cubana, and did some private-eye work on the side. But Nolan said it would be a waste of time and money because we didn't have enough information. And why did I want to find such an irresponsible and coldhearted person anyway?

I couldn't argue with that. As a child, I had kept up hope that my mother would return someday with a credible explanation for her long absence—explanations that ranged from her being sick or imprisoned to having ties with the CIA—until I accepted that she didn't care for me and never would. Afterward, whenever I thought of her, I ended up furious, but I still wanted a chance to ask her, face-to-face, why she had dropped me like a hot potato.

Mamina had taken her place, raising me and giving me all the love that I needed and more. She kept me fed and clothed during the "special period," the economic crisis that had peppered the nineties with rationings and blackouts. Thanks to her, I never missed my mother. But now I missed *her*.

After marrying Nolan, I visited Mamina at least once a year, usually at Christmas. She was delighted that we were coming back earlier this time. There was a bag of gifts for her in my suitcase—chocolate bars, Hershey's Kisses, Florida Water, housecoats, Palmolive soap, multivitamins and Spanish-language magazines. I sent her money too, but these were treats she couldn't buy in Havana. I also brought hair curlers and a compact for her best friend, Catalina.

Mamina lived in our old home, which had been my father's. Though it had fallen into disrepair, passersby often stopped to admire the Art Deco design of the building. It even had a name, Villa Santa Marta, written in elegant wrought-iron letters over the gate, and was located in Miramar, a posh, tree-lined neighborhood. But my grandma missed her old ranch in Pinar del Río, where her niece and nephew lived. Her only friend in Havana was Catalina, who lived alone as well because her daughter, Yaima, had married an old Spaniard and moved to Galicia with him.

Truth be known, Yaima was a *jinetera*. A few years older than me, she used to walk up and down Malecón Avenue in miniskirts and high heels. "A fast girl," Mamina would say.

A *jinetera* I wasn't. Just a flirt, Julia said. Heartless, Lorenzo had called me. I remembered our last encounter, those precious, defining minutes that changed my whole life. The crushed gardenias and the awkward, undignified manner in which I fled.

Get out of my head!

NOLAN AND I BOARDED the ship on deck three and found ourselves in the lobby, welcomed by tuxedoed waiters offering free cocktails. Nolan wrinkled his nose. I took a sip of a pink mix: it had grenadine, rum and something else. Something sweet. Condensed milk? Whatever, it was good.

On a stage, which was carpeted and skirted in red, a band played Buena Vista Social Club's *"El cuarto de Tula."*

It was actually a sad song about a poor woman whose room got burned down because she went to sleep and forgot to put out a candle, but the rhythm was lively and upbeat. My shoulders moved as I hummed under my breath "*y no apagó la vela.*" I was having fun until a question struck me: Had Lorenzo really forgotten to put out his candle, like Tula, that fateful night?

Lorenzo again! *¡Carajo!* I threw the thought far away and tried to focus on my surroundings.

The *Narwhal* looked like a hotel, only nicer than most hotels I had ever been in. My shoes sank into a thick purple rug. There were plush sofas and loveseats around marble-top tables. Gleaming chandeliers. A baby grand in a corner. I didn't want to ooh and aah like a bumpkin, but I was impressed.

The ship's photographer asked if we wanted professional photos taken. Nolan declined. He wasn't looking too photogenic with his hair sticking out and his general air of fatigue and misery.

The loudspeakers announced that all cabins were ready.

"Let's go, Mercy," Nolan said. "I'm exhausted."

OUR STATEROOM WAS ON deck nine. In the hall we got to meet our next-door neighbors, a couple in their late sixties. The woman was a faded blonde. The man had a salt-and-pepper goatee and slicked-back hair that made him look like an aged Don Juan. They kept fumbling with the card and inserting it into the slot in what seemed to be the wrong way.

"They don't call me Technophobe Tim for nothing," the guy said apologetically after Nolan helped them open the door.

"What ever happened to run-of-the-mill keys?" the woman grumbled. "Why is everything electronic these days?"

They both carried Louis Vuitton luggage, and I remembered what Candela had said about "older people with disposable income." If that was the case, Nolan and I would feel out of place, and so would Selfa. But don't look a gift horse in the mouth, right? I reminded myself that it was a *free* trip.

Our cabin was big and airy, with wood walls, two sofa beds, two nightstands, a closet with sliding doors and a white leather armchair. A bucket of ice and an elegant crystal carafe had been placed on the dresser. There were Godiva chocolates and welcoming cards on the sofa beds.

"We're getting quite the VIP treatment," Nolan said.

I smiled at the woman in the mirror. My hair had been recently cut into a layered bob. My white dress made my tanned skin glow. Despite having woken up at an unholy hour, I still looked good. Most importantly, I *felt* good, my ridiculous fears banished. I turned around. Nolan was behind me.

"It's perfect for a fresh start, *papito*." I caressed his left cheek, my smile now playful.

He moved one step away. I backed off too, hurt. So much for our second honeymoon!

The flat-screen television showed a live webcam of the ship alternating with the next day's schedule: arriving in Havana at 7 A.M., disembarking at 9 A.M., guided tour of the Cathedral at 10 A.M., lunch from noon to 1 P.M. and an optional visit to El Capitolio at 2 P.M. There were evening events as well, but I didn't pay attention. My plan was to spend most of the day with Mamina while Nolan gave his lecture and met with Doctor Fernández.

There were two blue mesh chairs and a round table on the balcony. I sat outside to enjoy the breeze and the bay view. Nolan headed to the bathroom. His back curved as he walked. He looked sad. Defeated. Despite the sting of his recent rejection, I felt sorry for him.

6: Doctor Spivey

Candela had asked me repeatedly if I "really" loved Nolan. She thought I had hooked up with him just to get out of Cuba. *No jodas, chica,* I always said. Had that been the case, why would I have stayed married to him all these years?

Yes, I hadn't forgotten Lorenzo, but he had died a long time ago. Despite the age difference, Nolan and I made a good couple. I liked the fact that he could talk about almost anything—even if, at times, he talked for too long. After we had finally tied the knot, I never questioned his love. "You are the best thing that has ever happened to me," he had said many times. He was an even-tempered man, unlike Lorenzo, who had a short fuse. On the flip side, Nolan was too passive and afraid of change. Fear had probably been behind his reluctance to divorce his first wife and, later, to leave Point South College after the writing on the wall became clear.

Ours was never a passionate love affair—well, maybe at first, when we were sneaking behind Lorenzo's back. Save for those few days in Cuba, we didn't even have a real courtship. After I moved to Miami and transitioned from Merceditas to Mercy, we had had to deal with his children, who wouldn't talk to him for a long time. (Katy, *la malcriada*, still hated my guts, though the boy, Kayden, had slowly warmed up to me.) But all in all, after nine years, we had never had any major disagreement. We would make it, I thought. We were going through a rough patch, but doesn't every couple, at some point?

Lorenzo had introduced us in 2006. Nolan used to take his students for four-week summer courses at the Faculty of Arts and Letters, where people called him "Doctor Spivey." He was working on a book about Cuba's socialist realism, his research focused on an author named Manuel Cofiño, who—Lorenzo claimed, with great irritation—imitated Russian Nobel Prize winner Mikhail Sholokhov.

All of that interested me less than the pictures "Doctor Spivey" had stored in his laptop: a manicured backyard with a swimming pool and a red barbecue, and a Parisian café where he had stopped with his wife and kids a few months back. (The wife, a tall and portly blonde, looked like a stuck-up cow.) That was some life, not what Lorenzo and I had.

Nolan had once mentioned his salary, sixty-five thousand dollars a year, an amount that sounded like a million to me. Suddenly Lorenzo, with his squalid peso wages, became much less appealing. I began to dream of a modern house and the exotic vacations my current boyfriend couldn't afford. Wasn't I half-American myself? I belonged in La Yuma, as we called the United States. I was wasting my time here in Cuba, where there weren't many opportunities whether you went to college or not.

There was more—I wasn't *that* mercenary. Nolan was a handsome guy, a couple years older than Lorenzo and not as tall, but well preserved. His eyes sparkled when he looked at me. He was so in love with me that he was willing to leave everything behind so we could start over, together, a new life. In a much better place than where destiny—and my runaway mother's decision—had placed me.

IN NOVEMBER 2007, WHILE Lorenzo was still in prison because of the book issue, I traveled to Miami with a student visa that Nolan helped me get. Ostensibly, I was going to take a literature workshop at Florida

International University, though I never had plans to set foot in a classroom. I suggested he get me a fiancée visa, but there were many obstacles. The biggest one being that he was still married.

Mamina, who had doted on Lorenzo, wasn't pleased with Nolan. "*Mija*, if that guy were really interested in you, he would have left his wife," she had said. "Besides, it was wrong of him to take you away from your boyfriend."

"He didn't take me away!" I protested. "I left Lorenzo of my own free will. Relationships don't always work."

"Lorenzo's a good man. But that Nolo . . . I don't know what to think of him."

I did. He was a softie. It had been so easy to seduce him, to make him forget he even had a wife. There was nothing to fear. He was crazy for me and would come around.

Nolan had told me he needed time to end his marriage in a proper manner. He assured me that Lou Ellen knew about our relationship and was okay with it. They just had to divide up their finances and break the news to the kids, especially the girl, who was at a difficult age. Katy was then fifteen, five years younger than me.

When I arrived, little suitcase with a couple of dresses in hand, Nolan hadn't yet divorced Lou Ellen, but had rented a place where I could "temporarily" stay. Not a nice house like his. Not a luxury condo in Coral Gables or Miami Beach, as I had expected. (I was so painfully naïve.) My new home was an efficiency in Hialeah. Smaller than my bedroom, even smaller than the servants' quarters in our Miramar home.

I withered in that hot, ugly room with no car and no money, only five hundred dollars Nolan had given me. (The first week I spent half on groceries and the other half on clothes after discovering a nearby mall.) He kept finding excuses to not go out together, dropping by in the afternoons after his classes to make quick love and run. In the meantime, he inadvertently disclosed that Lou Ellen also worked at the university. He saw her every day, at home *and* on campus, and they hadn't been able to "divide finances" yet?

To make things worse, Nolan left to attend a four-day symposium in Arkansas or Alabama or *casa del carajo*. I had been in the country just a few weeks, didn't know a soul in Miami, and he needed to travel right away? He didn't care I was alone in that horrible place with no one to talk to.

Two whole days after his return, he had only called

me once. One morning I woke up on the wrong side of the bed, found out which bus passed near the Florida International University campus and got there after a two-hour trip. I located the Spanish Department and asked the secretary for Doctor Nolan Spivey, *por favor*.

"Are you one of his students?" she asked.

"I am his fiancée."

The woman's mouth hung open. "Excuse me?"

"We met in Havana, and he's going to marry me," I answered, enunciating slowly to make sure she understood. We were speaking Spanish, which clearly wasn't her first language.

After the secretary recovered from the shock, she moused her way into an office. Soon other people scurried inside. Muffled conversations came through the closed door. Holding my head high, I sat on a couch that faced the room where the gossip fest was taking place and waited for Nolan to show up—

Ah, he was the biggest *llorón* I'd ever met! He cried when I exposed him in front of his colleagues. He must have cried when he *did* have to tell the truth to his wife and children. And he cried on the day we finally got married in March 2008, while the justice of the peace seemed intrigued and one of the witnesses (both were Nolan's graduate students) couldn't help sniffling herself.

I got to meet Lou Ellen, who turned out *not* to be a stuck-up cow at all. She had a thick Southern accent, a toothy smile and flawless manners. But I was younger, prettier and had way more *sandunga*. No wonder Nolan had chosen me, I thought, convinced that I had won my first battle on American soil.

Like I said, I was more than a bit naïve.

Lou Ellen and Nolan shared custody of the kids, an arrangement that made my life miserable two weeks out of the month. As part of the divorce deal, she kept their former home, barbecue and everything else. We rented a small, ordinary house not far from the campus, with a concrete backyard and no swimming pool.

We had been married a little over two years when Nolan left Florida International University. His divorce was a big scandal in their little tight-knit academic world. All the women in the Spanish Department, which was almost entirely composed of women, had sided with Lou Ellen and shunned him. He took a nontenured job at Point South College that offered less money and prestige and we moved to Coldwood Condos in Gainesville. He had given up a lot for our relationship. But so had I.

NOW HERE HE WAS, still in the shower! At first it seemed like he was talking to himself, then I realized he was crying.

A mist carried by the ocean breeze moistened my cheeks. Because I couldn't be crying, of course! *I* wasn't a *llorona*. After quietly wiping my face, I stood up and paced up and down the balcony, staring at the small waves that crashed against the ship.

7: The One-Trick Pony

As I gazed at the restless blue waters, it dawned on me that many of Lorenzo's friends, or so-called friends, had a streak of bad luck after his death. Look at Selfa, losing her son and now working a menial job. Look at Nolan, depressed and unemployed. I wondered how Javier Jurado, Lorenzo's literary agent, had fared. As a writer, Javier had had only one success, a novel that won the Saint Jordi award in Spain. The novel was *Las Perseidas*, published under *his* name with a different title.

Javier freelanced for travel magazines and was doing a feature on Old Havana's Cathedral Square when someone suggested he interview Lorenzo Alvear, who knew so much about the city. They began talking about books—of course—and the Spaniard mentioned he had started a career as a literary agent. Lorenzo was elated after the guy read his manuscript and agreed to represent it. Though he hadn't made a sale yet, Javier lived in Barcelona, "Spain's publishing hub." He was friends with well-known editors. He had to be the real deal! (For all his intellect, Lorenzo could be rather naïve too.) I didn't like the journalist or agent or whatever he claimed to be—a mousy guy who didn't look people in the eye. Then it turned out that he was *also* a writer. He'd once published a book that, he admitted, had tanked. That was why he had resorted to selling other people's work.

Javier sent Lorenzo's novel to the Saint Jordi contest in January 2007 and heard—unofficially—that the book was going to be a finalist. Even if it didn't win anything, that was still big for a new author. Besides, one of the contest's judges, a publisher, had shown interest in the novel. He might end up buying it! When Javier brought the good news to Havana, The Viking took everybody to celebrate at El Floridita restaurant. We ate lobster, got drunk and toasted to success and literary fame.

"To *Las Perseidas*!"

The title came from the Perseid meteor shower and acted as a metaphor, Lorenzo said. A metaphor for what, I never understood.

That dinner at El Floridita was the last time that the four of us were together. Shortly afterward I had a stupid fling with Kiel. A few weeks later, in the summer of 2007, Nolan returned from Miami and our affair began.

In the meantime, Lorenzo told a few colleagues at the Faculty of Arts and Letters about the book and the Saint Jordi contest. Selfa asked Javier to represent her novel, but the Spaniard declined. And then Lorenzo was arrested—

Since we had already broken up, I didn't call, much less visit him. Wrong on my part, but after the political police questioned me, I thought it wise to keep my distance. I was preparing my move to Miami and didn't want anything to interfere with it. I was also busy with the exit permit, the American visa and—ah, excuses, excuses. I've never forgiven myself for being so cold-hearted. *Just like my mother*, I thought.

I was already in Miami when someone told me that Kiel's friend, the old-guard general, had helped get Lorenzo out of prison. Relieved, I went to La Ermita de la Caridad and thanked Our Lady of Charity. And I'm not even Catholic. I hoped that his novel would get published and he'd become a famous writer. I honestly wanted the best for him.

But there would be no happy ending. Shortly after his release, Lorenzo burned himself to death in his apartment. The official version was that he went to sleep leaving a candle unattended. The fire had spread fast because Lorenzo's huge collection of books had fed it, his next-door neighbors claimed.

But it didn't ring true. Lorenzo could have, at least, cried for help. How come his neighbors didn't hear *anything*? Some said he committed suicide, though that didn't make sense either. He had been vindicated and was about to have his job back, plus a formal apology. He still had his novel to look forward to. Was it because of me? (Ah, those crushed gardenias. The blue shadows under his eyes.) But we had broken up several months before.

After a while, I stopped trying to figure it out. If I was going to start a new life, the old one had to be left behind with those who had once been part of it.

Around a year later, already married to Nolan, I was listening to the WQBA when I recognized Javier's voice. Old Javier, who had won the Saint Jordi award with a novel called *Light in Transit*. The Saint Jordi award? I kept listening and found out he was presenting the book at the Miami Book Fair. At the end of the program he read an excerpt that sounded suspiciously like *Las Perseidas*. I hadn't had the patience to finish the four-hundred-page manuscript, but remembered enough from what Lorenzo had told me to recognize the plot and some characters. Javier had only changed the title.

I wanted to call the WQBA station and tell the truth, but Nolan wouldn't let me, afraid of a lawsuit. "Here you don't go around making such allegations if you can't prove them, Mercy!" There was no way of proving anything. Lorenzo had once given a public reading of *Las Perseidas* at a venue called La Madriguera, but I didn't remember who had been there—a bunch of writerly types I never saw again. And he was dead. He didn't have any family left. Who was I, an ex-girlfriend who had dumped him for another man, to go to battle for his literary legacy? I already had enough trouble with Nolan's kids and didn't need more stress. I let it go but hated Javier for his betrayal. It was much worse than mine.

Not long after that I saw the novel at Books & Books in Coral Gables, where I had gone with Nolan. The cover featured a shower of stars splashed like confetti over a dark-blue sky. Below was the Havana Bay with the Morro Castle on one side. I opened it. *Light in Transit* by Javier Jurado. I sighed and put it back on the shelf . . .

NOLAN CAME OUT OF the shower and sat on his sofa bed with a pained expression. I tried to say something nice but couldn't, still thinking of Lorenzo, Javier, the book. Suddenly, I realized why the guy with the European Union passport had looked so *familiar*.

I took out my cellphone and googled Javier Jurado. In a 2013 *El País* article he complained that his most recent novel didn't sell because it wasn't just like the previous one. "People want me to keep writing *Light in Transit* over and over, but that's not possible. In a way, I am victim of my own success." His *own* success? *¡Sinvergüenza!* I scrolled down and found more articles. The reviewers lambasted his other novels. One called Javier a one-trick pony.

A one-book thief, that's what he was.

Nolan skimmed through a glossy information booklet, mumbling about a safety drill. I kept trying to find a current photo of Javier. Finally, there was one. He was older. Thinner. And identical to the man I had just seen.

But Javier lived in Barcelona. Why would he go to Havana on a cruise—from Miami, of all places? It couldn't be him. Talking to Selfa must have unearthed painful memories and started giving me delusions.

"Let's go get something to eat," I told Nolan.

"I'd rather rest until the muster drill starts."

"The what drill?"

"The safety drill, Mercy. Where we learn what to do and where to go if there's an evacuation. Our muster station is the library, on deck seven."

"Fine. I'm going to find a snack. I'm starving."

"Have fun."

He looked so downcast that I almost changed my mind and stayed with him, but I was too curious about Javier. I was also nervous, unable to shake off a sense of impending doom.

8: Macarena

The casino and all shops remained closed while the ship was in port. People had gathered on deck twelve around an outdoor bar or inside the various pools and hot tubs. A gaggle of kids threw a big inflatable doll into the ocean and ran away laughing. Signs in several languages read DO NOT THROW ANYTHING OVERBOARD, but a life-sized plastic mermaid and other smaller toys were already riding the waves. Music floated in the salty air, the first lines of my favorite Los del Rio song.

It had been popular in Havana when I was a teenager—even musical hits arrived late to the Cuban scene. Girls my age danced like Macarena. Moved like Macarena. We all wanted to be like her, though she wasn't precisely a role model, having cheated on her boyfriend with two different guys who happened to be his buddies. She dreamed of shopping in fashion stores and living in New York. (Didn't we all?) Whenever our friends left their partners for guys who had more money or status (ones who often happened to be foreigners), we called it "the Macarena effect."

I sang along without thinking until it got to Macarena saying, "Now, come on, what was I supposed to do? He was out of town and his two friends were so fine."

His two friends *were* so fine.

The live band was surrounded by enthusiastic, if not exactly skilled, dancers. Some couples, most of them gray-haired, sunbathed on the lounge chairs. Others stayed wisely in the shaded areas, umbrella drink in hand. The Devilfish Bar was packed. There was also a restaurant, Maelstrom, but it hadn't opened yet.

I searched the crowd for Javier's look-alike, hoping Selfa wasn't around with her baggage of fear and sadness. Not to be insensitive, but dealing with Nolan's depression was more than enough.

Thankfully, I didn't see Selfa anywhere. And then my luck continued because I spotted the guy who had looked so familiar before. He stood against the railing with his back to the sea, wearing a Miami Dolphins T-shirt. I compared him with the newspaper photos and my suddenly awakened memories and concluded it *wa*s Javier Jurado. Like Selfa, he had changed, only that instead of getting fatter, he was skinnier and more leathery. But there was no room for doubt. It was the one-trick pony, the book thief himself.

He didn't see me until I stopped firmly in front of him.

"Merceditas!" he yelped. "What are you doing here?"

His thick Castilian accent was the only thing about him that had remained the same. I ignored the question—what could anyone be doing aboard a cruise ship, *estúpido*?—and just watched him squirm.

"Are you on vacation?" he asked again.

So he was pursuing this idiotic line of inquiry. I threw it back at him. "Are you?"

He smiled. "It's more like a workation. I've been invited by Casa de las Américas."

A Cuban cultural institution with its own well-known literary prize had invited Javier? He must have fared better than the rest of us.

"It's been a while since . . ." he went on, stammering, "since I've gotten this kind of attention."

I listened, hands on my hips.

"But my time has come again."

"*Again*, Javier? The first time was when you published Lorenzo's novel as your own, huh?"

His face contorted. He swallowed and looked down. "I don't know what you're talking about."

But he did. His Adam's apple bobbed.

"I'm talking about *Las Perseidas*!" I said, louder than I had to. "Did you really think nobody was going to find out?

"Others did worse," Javier croaked.

"What do you mean by that?" I snapped.

He hung his head and said nothing.

"You stole the book, *cabrón*!"

"You are right."

His eyes finally met mine.

"But no publisher would have touched a first novel by an unknown dead man," he added, his voice a squeak. "The award would have gone to someone else. The judges knew me, though, and I wanted to give the manuscript a chance."

"You wanted to give *yourself* a chance. You made a lot of money with that book!"

"And it ruined my writing career because I was never able to match it. Publishers kept waiting for me to write another bestseller, but I didn't have Lorenzo's talent." Javier turned his palms up in a gesture of defeat. "I did something wrong, yes, and paid dearly for it."

It could have been an act. But he also could have

denied the whole thing or called onboard security on me for harassing him and making a scene in front of everyone. People were looking at us as it was already.

"Sorry, Javier," I whispered. "I don't know what just got into me. I shouldn't have called you a thief, much less a *cabrón*."

"I've called myself all that and worse, Merceditas. I *did* know I was going to be found out someday. Better by you than anybody else."

The book was history. It had been for a long time. I was taking things out on Javier because I was mad at myself. About Lorenzo. Leaving him, letting him die. Because I had never gotten over him in my heart.

"Let's go have a mojito, Javier."

He still walked with the limp I had noticed at the entry queue. At the Devilfish Bar, I put the drinks on my onboard tab because he made no move to pay for them. Lorenzo used to say the Spaniard was a cheapskate.

My mojito was watery and bland without *yerbabuena*, which, no matter what Americans say, isn't the same as spearmint.

To ease the tension, I asked Javier about his life. He said that he was living in Miami but didn't elaborate. I told him about Nolan and the lecture he was going to give at the University of Havana.

"Oh, you married a college professor?"

"Yes."

"American?"

I nodded. It seemed like he didn't know our story. He was in Barcelona when Lorenzo and I had broken up and I doubted that Lorenzo had volunteered any particulars later. They hadn't been *that* close.

"What does he teach?"

"Literature."

"What kind?"

I shrugged. "Magical realism, socialist realism, dirty realism, *lo real maravilloso* . . ."

"That's great!"

His excitement sounded inflated. But he was a writer, albeit a bad one. All things literary probably got him going.

"Cultural exchanges with Havana are now more popular than ever." He gulped and blushed. "Cuba sells like hotcakes. Magazines, books, tours . . . If you don't mind my asking, is it a well-paid gig?"

"*Ay*, Javier, please. The University of Havana wouldn't even reimburse my husband's airfare."

"At least Casa de las Américas paid for my cruise. I couldn't have come otherwise."

That didn't seem right.

"Wouldn't it have been cheaper for them to buy you a plane ticket?" I asked.

"They want me to get acquainted with this ship because we're working on a deal." He flicked an eyebrow. "Casa has partnered with Nautilus to promote creative writing cruises through their people-to-people program. They offered me a job teaching workshops on board."

"Casa partnered with an *American* cruise company?"

"Yes. Things are changing under Raúl Castro. And Nautilus isn't an American company. Nominally, at least."

Things were changing, but not that fast. Casa de las Américas was the Cuban government's most important cultural institution. Even if they were to do business with a cruise line, hundreds of *Cuban* writers were Casa members. Why hire someone from Spain to teach a workshop? Why give him a free cruise? Like those "free tickets" Selfa and I had gotten—

And, just like that, it hit me. Selfa. Javier. Nolan. Myself. We all had crossed paths before. Selfa and Nolan could have met at the Faculty of Arts and Letters. Javier and Nolan had visited Lorenzo and possibly ran into each other in his apartment. Selfa had sent her book to Javier. Lorenzo was the thread connecting us.

"Did you ever meet Selfa Segarra, Javier?"

"The name doesn't ring a bell."

"A professor at the Faculty of Arts and Letters."

His face remained blank. "I never met any of Lorenzo's colleagues."

"She wanted you to represent her book."

He pinched his eyebrows. Was he trying to remember or getting ready to lie?

"Lorenzo gave me a novel on behalf of a friend," he said at last, "but didn't introduce me to the author. I turned it down."

I was looking for a way to bring up Selfa's presence there and connect all the dots when Javier took my hand and squeezed it.

"Thank you, Merceditas," he whispered. "Thank you so much."

"Oh, uh, you're welcome. The mojitos weren't that good, though."

"No, I mean, thank you for not telling anybody—you could have caused a big stink and gotten me in trouble over that book."

I almost did, was my instinctual response. But the anger was gone now, diluted like the rum in our mediocre mojitos.

"At least your title was better," I tried to joke.

"*Light in Transit* sounds better than *Las Perseidas*, at least to me."

"Ah, Merceditas. The phrase wasn't even mine. I got it from him too."

Before I could make any comment, an alarm went off.

"All passengers, please collect your life jackets and proceed to your muster stations as indicated on the back of your stateroom door," said a voice from the ship's loudspeakers. "The mandatory safety drill will start in ten minutes."

"Believe me, I really wish I hadn't—" Javier sighed. "But it is over. *Lo pasado, pisado*, don't you think?"

Let bygones be bygones. Spanish is more colorful: step on the past.

"I guess so."

"Let's get together again. I'd like to meet your husband."

Maybe you already have, I thought, but didn't say it. Why the insistence, anyway? I still didn't trust Javier.

PART II:
What Happens on Ship

1: Libraries

After Javier left to look for his own meeting place, I felt the impulse to flee—we hadn't sailed yet—and forget the trip, Selfa, the Spaniard, even Nolan. Something was wrong. Or was it?

Raúl Castro had allowed cruises in Cuba (with Cubans on board!) for the first time in sixty years. He had built private marinas and five-star hotels for foreigners. Tourism was one of the island's main sources of income. Casa de las Américas could recruit authors who had once had their fifteen minutes of fame, like Javier, pay them a few bucks to teach writing courses and pocket most of the money.

I stepped out of the elevator too soon and ended up on deck eight. As I took the stairs down there was a tingling on my neck, like a subtle vibration. The feeling of being watched crept over me. I turned around. But nobody seemed to be paying attention to me. People were rushing to their meeting places while two crewmembers stood in the hall, offering directions to the frazzled latecomers.

A group had gathered in a small room that I assumed was the library. When I came in, a uniformed guy was calling out, "Mr. Ostargó? Kiel Ostargó?"

I had started looking for Nolan, but hearing what appeared to be The Viking's full name brought me to a full pause.

"Is Mr. Ostargó here, please?"

No one answered. The drill manager glanced at the list again and turned to me. "Are you at your proper muster station, madam?"

"Is this the library?"

"We are in the conference room, madam. The library is around the corner."

I didn't want to leave before taking a good look at "Mr. Ostargó." It couldn't be Kiel. Of course it couldn't. I had probably misunderstood, or the names were just similar. Still, it made me nervous. *More* nervous. I pretended to be distracted but the drill manager addressed me again.

"You should go to your muster station, madam."

I left, reluctantly, and got in the library when the drill was about to begin. Nolan stood in a corner with our life jackets in hand.

"Where were you?"

"Ah, having a mojito."

He frowned.

I put on the orange life jacket, which smelled like plastic and glue.

Our drill manager was a young woman whose nametag read ALICIA. She had a pretty face and shiny, shoulder-length black hair. After crossing my name off a list, she went over the evacuation procedures and related blah-blah.

While she talked, I kept looking out to the hall in case "Mr. Ostargó" passed by. He didn't. Feeling both bored and edgy, I started to inspect the room. The *Narwhal* library was warm and elegant with its built-in bookshelves, lamps with glass shades and brown leather armchairs. But there was only a handful of books, and I couldn't help but think again of Lorenzo's large collection. Even if I wasn't much of a reader, I had always liked libraries.

LORENZO AND I HAD had our first date at the Biblioteca Nacional José Martí. I had asked him for help with a paper—an old trick, but it worked—and he suggested we meet at the National Library, where they had some materials I should be studying for our class. His hands were large but elegant, with neatly clipped nails. They moved smoothly over the pages, pointing to paragraphs while I pretended to take notes.

Unfortunately (or fortunately), they didn't have a certain volume that he wanted me to consult.

"Would you like to stop by my apartment?" he asked. "It's very small, but I have almost as many books as the library."

I must have looked horrified because he laughed and said it was a joke. Not really. When we got there, I found books in the living area, in the bedroom, even in the tiny attic he had built, taking advantage of the high ceilings. He was particularly fond of Alexandre Dumas's works, which occupied an entire shelf: *The Count of Monte Cristo*, *The Three Musketeers*, *Twenty Years After* . . . We didn't open any, of course, and I didn't leave until the next day . . .

When I returned home, Mamina had been furious. I had never spent the night out of the house without letting her know in advance.

"Couldn't you have given me a call at least, *niña*? I was worried to death!"

"I forgot because I'm in love," was my excuse.

That was how it all began.

"WHY DO YOU READ so much when you can watch the movies?" I had asked Lorenzo once. "That's such a waste of time!"

He got incensed and called me *burra*. But I wasn't dumb, much less a donkey, just not interested in the same things he was. After all, we were fifteen years apart.

Books were Lorenzo's life and world, and it had been hard for him to accept that other people didn't share his passion. He used to call me a lazy reader, which wasn't as bad as *burra* and maybe close to the truth.

"DURING EMERGENCY EVACUATION, PASSENGERS can board the lifeboats following the established route—"

The drill manager was still giving her spiel and brought me out of thoughts of Lorenzo. I had missed the lifeboats' location but figured it wasn't too important. Most people weren't paying attention anyway. Technophobe Tim was busy examining a nautical chart of the Bahamas that covered half a wall while his wife looked at a detailed model of the *Narwhal* inside a glass display case.

A heavy bronze bust of some writer or poet was perched on the top shelf of a bookcase. I had seen that frowning dude before but couldn't remember where, or who he was. Sculptures and portraits of famous people ought to include their names to make it easier for regular folks like me to identify them.

The drill ended. Nolan took me by the arm. His hand was cold and clammy.

"I hope to hear from Doctor Fernández before we disembark tomorrow," he said as we walked out of the library. "I still don't know if he's picking us up at the terminal or expects me to meet him later. Now that I think about it, his last message was a bit . . . vague. God, I hope he doesn't blow me off after we've come all the way from Gainesville."

"At least we're on a free cruise," I said on autopilot, then remembered Selfa, who had gotten one too. And "Mr. Ostargó!"

I took a long, deep breath and considered telling Nolan about Selfa and The Viking, but then I would have had to bring up Lorenzo too. There was no way around it.

"There's a buffet restaurant on the pool deck," I said instead. "It'll be open soon. Do you want to try it?"

"I'm not hungry." His eyes were reddish, and his face, pale and puffy, looked like a watery moon. "Sorry, Mercy, but I need to lie down for a while."

"You drove more than six hours this morning,

papito." I gave him a peck on the cheek. "We got up early. Why don't you take a nap?"

"That may help."

He shuffled back to the cabin—head down and shoulders slumped. He didn't need to be worried about a couple of incidents that my imagination was probably blowing way out of proportion.

Alone, I wandered around the carpeted hall, discreetly scanning people's faces. Meeting Selfa there could have been a coincidence; meeting Javier was pushing it. If it turned out that The Viking was on board as well . . . The idea sent shudders down my spine. Then I remembered Candela's advice—*estate tranquila*—and did my best to relax.

The ship's business center was at the end of the hall. It was small, with only five computers and a printer arranged around a circular counter. The only user was Grateful Dead, who startled and closed the page he was looking at when I came in.

"I can't open my email on my phone," he said, almost apologetically. As if I cared.

There was a window with the curtains opened. The rippling of the waves reflected on the ceiling. A travel magazine displayed on the counter featured the University of Havana on its cover. I leafed through it.

There was a long article about the success of *casas particulares* (private homes that host tourists) in Havana.

Lorenzo had once planned to turn his apartment into a *casa particular*. His two rooms and the attic put together weren't over six hundred square feet, but what the place lacked in size was made up by the location, near Paseo del Prado and perfect for a short-term tourist rental.

Cathedral Square, El Floridita, the Morro Castle with its popular firing-of-the-canon ceremony and the Bellas Artes Museum were all within walking distance. El Paladar de Carmela, a private restaurant, was on the same block. Carmela catered to tourists, and all the neighboring *casa particular* owners sent their clients there. Lorenzo would offer his guests private tours. He knew the city up and down, every nook, corner, street and little *callejón* of it. He used to joke that if he had a daughter, he would name her Habana . . .

I noticed the tears rolling down my face when they reached my mouth and dissolved on my lips, leaving a salty coating. I wiped them and realized I was alone in the business center. Grateful Dead had left.

Looking up, I caught a glimpse of a shadow on the wall. For one terrifying moment, I thought I was being watched again. Hunted. Fear made my skin prickle. I bolted, but by the time I got to the door, there was nobody outside. The hall was empty. Just in case, I ran to the lobby and upstairs, back to deck twelve.

Once I was surrounded by smiling people and bright lights, with another Buena Vista Social Club song playing on the loudspeaker, my fears started to recede. More so, once it occurred to me that the "shadow" had likely been a reflection of the waves. I was making myself paranoid. *Pendeja.*

The incident, silly as it was, reminded me of something that had happened in late April, when Nolan was still working at Point South. We had had people over for dinner—three colleagues he had bonded with over their shared resentment of the college environment. I hated such social occasions. Conversations revolved around professors and students I didn't know and issues I didn't understand or care about, like books and politics. Besides, those middle-aged men and women spoke to me louder and slower than necessary.

They all liked Cuban food and I had chosen *ropa vieja*, though it meant explaining for the umpteenth time that the dish had nothing to do with old clothes. It was just shredded beef with vegetables—cubed carrots, tomatoes and celery and strips of red and yellow peppers that resembled an assortment of brightly colored rags.

Company had arrived and settled in the living room. I was in the kitchen, finishing the white rice to go with the *ropa vieja*, when a rustling of leaves in the backyard made me step outside. There was a shadow on the other side of the wall, but it moved away too fast for me to get a clear look. I didn't want to make a scene, so I had waited until our guests left to tell Nolan.

"Could it have been the wind, or a stray cat?" he asked. "Outsiders can't go past the security fence."

There had been no wind that evening. What I had seen seemed too big and humanlike to be a cat, and the security fence was a joke. I had forgotten my opener several times and all I had to do was wait for another car to go through the gate and then follow it.

Nolan and I had searched the backyard and walked around the common grounds with a flashlight. We found nothing. I had had to drop the issue but hadn't forgotten it . . .

Qué shadows *ni* shadows! My stomach growled. Like Mamina would say, *"El hambre hace ver visiones."* I was "seeing visions." After all, I had only eaten a light breakfast, and that had been almost ten hours ago.

2: The Beginning of the End

Cups and dishes clattered in Maelstrom, a buffet-style restaurant. The air, thick with the fragrance of sauces and stews, was filled with laughter and chatter. The buffet displayed a Cuban-style menu: rice with chicken, ham croquettes, black bean soup, roasted pork and fried plantains. I piled up my plate with *arroz con pollo* and secured a window table. The ship wasn't scheduled to leave until 5 P.M. and I looked longingly at the high-rises silhouetted against the sky.

Ah, Miami! If we had come a day earlier, as I'd wanted, we would have stopped at Versailles, the most famous Cuban restaurant in the city, for chicken-fried steak and a *cortadito*. Or we'd have gone to La Bakería Cubana and had a *flan de queso* or a piece of chocolate cake. But Nolan had refused, saying we didn't have money for a motel and six extra meals.

I loved Miami (Havana of the North, Candela called it) as much as I hated Gainesville with its Gators fans, hoity-toity college types, eternal mildew and the fact that the closest beach was two hours away. I wished to move back south, even if it meant Kendall or Hialeah, and live in a house that had a garden and trees instead of cramped in a condo with a postcard-sized yard.

Though the rice with chicken wasn't bad, it didn't taste like the dish I was used to. It lacked green peas, red peppers and lard. I picked at it, playing distractedly with the fork. The saffron-orange hue bled into the memories of another *arroz con pollo* meal that had changed my life.

IT WAS LATE MAY 2007 and finals week at the Faculty of Arts and Letters. Nolan was back in Havana and Lorenzo had invited him to have dinner with us in the "apartment." I was going to make my specialty: *arroz con pollo*, Mamina's recipe, always a hit among his foreign friends.

Nolan hadn't brought his students this time. When I wondered aloud why his wife and children hadn't come, seeing that it wasn't a business trip, Lorenzo said that American families didn't always travel in packs like we did.

"In the United States, couples sometimes take separate vacations and nobody finds it odd," he had said. "They just give each other space, which isn't a bad idea."

I would have argued this, but there were more pressing issues to deal with. Like the impossibility of feeding three people with half a breast and two slimy, scrawny thighs.

"How do you expect me to make *arroz con pollo* with no *pollo*?" I had whined after opening his bare refrigerator. "You should have waited until next week when we got our next ration card stuff!"

"Give him most of the chicken. We'll have an omelet or something afterward."

Though bad enough, missing the main ingredient hadn't been the only problem. We were out of saffron as well. Some people use turmeric instead, but it can't replicate the subtle aroma and floral flavor—saffron is what makes the rice and chicken good and true *arroz con pollo*. Besides, we didn't have turmeric either.

My concerns didn't register with Lorenzo; he had been too busy grading papers. When I had insisted, he told me to just cook "whatever" and stop pestering him.

"This is embarrassing! What's the *Americano* going to say?"

"What *can* he say? Intentions are what matters. We have limited resources, and he knows that."

Nolan's arrival had put an end to the argument. He had come early in case we needed anything from the tourists' shop. Before Lorenzo had a chance to speak (he would have said we needed nothing), I told "the *Americano*" that we were out of chicken. He offered to buy it, and also the saffron.

"Make sure you get the Spanish brand," I had added, emboldened by his good-natured smile and pretending not to notice Lorenzo's glare. "And a jar of green olives too, if you can find it."

"Why don't you guys come with me and get whatever you want?"

Lorenzo wouldn't hear of it.

"I have to post these grades tomorrow. You two go ahead. I'll be done when you're back."

Nolan and I took a government taxi to the Plaza Carlos III mall, where everything was sold in dollars or its Cuban equivalent, CUCs. I had felt nervous and wished my boyfriend had come along. What had happened with Kiel a few weeks before still haunted me. What a mistake that had been! Fortunately, Lorenzo didn't suspect a thing, I thought. He trusted me, but I didn't trust myself.

The ride had been short and uneventful. Nolan kept pointing to old buildings that had been renovated by

Eusebio Leal, saying they had been "preserved alive."
He didn't bring up his wife and children and I didn't
ask about them.

At the store, he bought not only two fat whole
chickens, saffron and olives, but also a jar of straw-
berry jam, a small ham, a loaf of bread and a bottle of
wine—more food than what Lorenzo got through his
ration card in a month. The grand total came close to
two hundred dollars. I was dismayed.

"It's my pleasure," Nolan had assured me. "Is there
anything else you'd like? Clothes, maybe? A gift for
your grandma?"

"Oh, goodness, no! Lorenzo will kill me!"

"We don't have to tell him. It'll be our secret."

We went together to several shops. He had insisted I
get something for myself, and I couldn't resist. Though
it all was rather innocent—the older, wealthier foreigner buying a present for his buddy's girlfriend—the
poisoned seed had been sown. I had been hurt by
the way Lorenzo had dismissed me early on and
couldn't help but notice the difference with Nolan.
My boyfriend asking me to make a meal out of air and
intentions, then telling me to go out with another guy
so he could finish grading his students' dull essays. And
his friend, generous and attentive, a true gentleman

who spent money without counting it. Actually, *all* his friends seemed to have more money than he did.

The memory of The Viking returned, making me squirm, but I pushed it back. That poor man was damaged, and not just physically. Nolan was nothing like him. Not that I was thinking of another betrayal but—

I had chosen a cubic zirconia bracelet and put it on right away. In another store, a pair of neon pink Lycra leggings caught my eye, and Nolan agreed (probably laughing to himself) that they were quite stylish.

At my suggestion, we returned in a red *almendrón*—a vintage Chevy. *Almendrones* charged dollars and were used generally by tourists. I had never ridden in one. I was elated, but as we got closer to Trocadero Street, where Lorenzo lived, my mood had begun to change. Being a guy, he wouldn't notice the bracelet, but the package with the flashy leggings would be difficult to hide. The purchase would mortify him. He had come to accept that his foreign friends paid for food since he couldn't afford it, but clothes for me? I think not.

I had shyly mentioned my concerns when sitting next to Nolan in the black leather back seat.

"Why don't you put the leggings on?"

I remember blushing at his question. "Won't that be weird?"

"Says who?"

I had been wearing a long skirt. Giggling, I shimmied into the leggings that were thusly concealed. The driver must have thought I was a *jinetera*. And at that moment, I had seen a flash of desire in Nolan's eyes.

The *almendrón* stopped in front of the building. Before we went upstairs, Nolan coughed and suggested we meet again the following day.

"Lorenzo, you and me?" I had asked, though I knew better.

"No, just you and me. Lorenzo's too busy—I know how stressful the end of the semester can get! But I can take you out to La Roca or Don Giovanni, or whichever restaurant you want."

Most people, Cubans and foreigners both, preferred privately owned *paladares*, but Nolan favored government-run restaurants.

"Okay," I said without thinking.

We went upstairs, I cooked for the three of us and my *arroz con pollo* turned out great. But I had lost my appetite. Part of me had known that going out with Nolan behind Lorenzo's back was wrong, even if nothing happened. Americans might do that in their country, but we were in Cuba, where engaged women didn't go out with other men. Period. Yet another part of me had been fed up with my boyfriend's "limited resources," and I couldn't help but glance at the zirconia bracelet's sheen.

This was The Viking all over again.

Nolan had picked me up the next day at my house in a blue *almendrón*. At La Roca, a nice enough government-run restaurant, we ordered steaks and mashed potatoes, shrimp cocktails, a shot of Havana Club 7 Años rum for him and a piña colada for me. We joked and talked about life in America while a band played the romantic ballad "*Quiéreme Mucho*." It had felt like a scene straight from a romance movie.

"How do you manage to look so beautiful all the time?" Nolan had whispered.

That had been the beginning of the end.

LA ROCA FADED TO Maelstrom. The lyrics of "*Quiéreme Mucho*" changed to a sweet-sounding, singsongy voice that said, "Ms. Selfa Segarra, your presence is required at the guest service desk."

The fork fell from my hand. I waited a few minutes but the announcement wasn't repeated.

The *arroz con pollo* was making me nauseous. I finished off the plantains and, still hungry, returned to the buffet. There was escargot served with garlic herb butter, which didn't look too appetizing. Nolan had told me that escargot was "an acquired taste." Fortunately, there were also big trays of *picadillo*— ground beef cooked with onions, potatoes, garlic and bell peppers—and I decided to give it a try, hoping it was more faithful to its Cuban roots than the *arroz con pollo*.

"Ms. Selfa Segarra, your presence is required *immediately* at the guest service desk!" The voice was less melodic this time and had an urgent undertone. It frightened me—but why? She might have just dropped her room card or her wallet.

My eyes searched the restaurant. I was still looking for Kiel, but nobody around resembled The Viking, and he wasn't exactly an ordinary-looking guy.

Back at my table with the *picadillo* and an ample serving of *congrí*—rice and black beans cooked together—I overheard a conversation between an older couple seated nearby. They were speaking Spanish, and I listened without intending to.

"What are you talking about?" the man said. "It was just kids throwing toys and other crap overboard."

"I saw the kids earlier, but this was different. It made a big splash, like a body. And I heard a woman crying for help."

"How could you have heard anything with that guy singing 'Macarena' at the top of his lungs?"

"Because I was on the lower deck, where they stow the lifeboats. It was quiet there, no loud music or anything. It was lonely and scary too, the perfect setting for a murder."

"You read too many mysteries, *vieja*."

"*Vieja*, me? No, *you're* the old man here. You're five years my senior!"

She slapped him playfully while he pretended to duck in fear. They were both laughing, but I had lost my appetite.

AFTER LEAVING THE RESTAURANT, I located the lifeboats in case there *was* an evacuation. They were stowed on deck five, a deserted and definitely ugly part of the ship. The walkway was narrow, and there were no chaise lounges, benches or any other places to sit. I didn't feel comfortable wandering about by myself and hurried back to the upper decks, where all the activity was.

A musical was about to start at the Bonaire Club on deck eleven. It was free and I got in.

The dancers were fabulous, performing everything from hip-hop and salsa to old rhythms like *paso doble* and foxtrot. A young Celia Cruz look-alike sang "*La Vida Es un Carnaval.*"

By the time the show ended, we had left the Miami port.

"We're sailing to Cuba!" a lady told me when we bumped into each other outside the theater.

"Woo-hoo!"

"There's a lecture about the building of the Morro Castle." She had a friendly, eager-to-please expression. "And then a free Spanish lesson in the library. Are you going? We can practice together."

"I don't think so, but thanks."

She looked disappointed. Maybe she was traveling by herself. "It's not fun to travel solo," Kiel had said the day I seduced him, a memory that still made my cheeks color with shame, not to mention remorse.

The damn Viking. He couldn't be on board. The cruise, with its educational bent, was designed for people who had never set foot on the island, which wasn't true in his case. Unless he'd gotten a free ticket as well? But he had too much money for that to have tempted him as it had me, Nolan and Selfa.

Selfa . . . Where was she anyway? I set out to find her while keeping on the lookout for Kiel, just in case. Again, I walked up and down the halls and ventured out to the decks, though making sure to be around people all the time. I circled the Devilfish Bar and the pools. *Nada.*

Back inside, I discovered that the boutiques were open. One can always count on shopping to help lift the mood. I bought a white cotton robe with the Nautilus logo for me and a blue pashmina shawl for Mamina. Everything was put on the onboard tab, which made spending easy.

The casino was nearby. A soft glow lit up the room, already full of serious, focused people. Tinkles and chirpings imitated coins clanking, but there was no real money anywhere. I stayed away because the slot machines looked like computers, devices I had never come to like. I didn't even own one, only using Nolan's when absolutely necessary. I'd never cared for Instagram, Twitter or other social media, and hadn't checked my email in weeks. I only started texting at Candela's insistence. She often said I was born in the wrong century; I wholeheartedly agreed.

Small groups were gathered around green velvet tables. Blackjack? Poker? I didn't know any card games, either. The place smelled like cigarette smoke, strong perfume and desperation. I kept walking.

A shimmering mini bottle of Kahlua Mudslide in

the liquor store window attracted me as much as the DUTY-FREE sign. I bought four, plus a full-sized bottle of Bacardí rum, and signed a sixty-dollar bill. The clerk wrapped everything up nicely but instead of handing me the package, he proceeded to explain that it would be put "on hold" until the last night of the cruise.

"What? You mean I can't take them back to my cabin?" I asked. Actually, I had planned to start with the Kahlua *before* reaching the room.

"No, madam, I'm sorry. You can't."

"Why is that?"

"Cruise regulations, madam. Our onboard alcohol policy—"

¡Mierda! I canceled the purchases and left the shop in a huff. Why would anybody want to wait until the end of the cruise to drink their overpriced booze?

A port talk was announced to discuss the next day's events and Nautilus's people-to-people protocols. They made it sound mandatory, but I ignored it. Nobody would tell me what to do, especially on vacation. I'd had enough of that in Cuba, where, as we used to say, "*Lo que no está prohibido es obligatorio.*" Whatever wasn't forbidden was compulsory.

Still, I stuck my head inside the theater while the port talk was taking place. As far as I could see, Selfa wasn't there. Neither was Kiel, or at least not The Viking—who knew about *the other* Kiel, the guy they'd been calling? Maybe it wasn't him at all. Kiel Ostargó could be a common name in Scandinavia, like Juan Pérez in Cuba . . . or the last name Fernández, now that I thought about it. I wondered if Nolan had even bothered to research the man who'd invited him to speak at the university. But he probably knew him from his previous trips. Though he had stopped taking his students to Havana after he left FIU (Point South College didn't care for such exchanges), he must have kept some contacts there.

When I finally made it to our cabin, Nolan was asleep, his face covered by a pillow. I got under the shower and began to whistle *"La Vida Es un Carnaval."*

Refreshed and calmer now, I put on my new robe, went out on the balcony and looked out at the ocean. Miami was no longer visible. Water surrounded us, a blue immensity rising and falling in its own secret rhythm. Streaks of gold and violet followed the sun as it sank into the horizon.

I soaked in the view that in some twisted way made me think of The Viking again. He used to travel a lot, and likely still did, even if he didn't visit Cuba anymore. But maybe he would, to see the old general and other established friends there. He must have been quite sad to hear Lorenzo had passed away. They were best friends; Lorenzo had once told me that The Viking was the closest thing he'd ever had to a brother.

My cringeworthy encounter with Kiel hadn't affected their friendship because Lorenzo never suspected anything. Yet that absurd and unconsummated affair had been the first link in the chain of events that had killed my relationship with Lorenzo. And, ultimately, I feared, killed *him*.

3: The Last Supper

Nolan looked much better when he woke up. His color had returned and he stood up straight. It was a quarter to eight, and the schedule on our TV screen informed us that a Cuban movie night would take place at nine o'clock as part of the cultural activities program.

"Do you want to go?" he asked.

"Sure."

It didn't say which movie would be featured. I'd heard that *Sergio and Sergei*, directed by Ernesto Daranas, had been released a few weeks ago in Havana, though it wasn't yet available on Netflix. It was the story of a Russian astronaut who was forgotten in space while perestroika swept through his country. I'd grown up hearing about perestroika—which at first I'd imagined to be a grumpy old Russian lady—and Daranas was my favorite Cuban director. Maybe we would be treated to a showing of his new film.

We took the elevator to deck ten, where the theater was located next to a restaurant called Nemo's Table. I wasn't hungry, but agreed when Nolan suggested we have dinner first. *He* needed to eat. And I could always make room in my stomach for something sweet and tasty.

The walls at Nemo's Table were decorated with Impressionist-style paintings—that much I recalled from my art history classes. Soft light came from silver globes that looked as if they were floating in the air all across the ceiling. The place was a classier venue than Maelstrom. But Nolan panicked for a minute, suspecting it was "a specialty restaurant," which meant we had to pay.

"So what?" I whispered. "It won't break us."

"We are in no position to throw away money, dear."

Thankfully, the hostess assured him that Nemo's Table was included in our free dining package, then led us to a table with an ocean view. There wasn't a lot to see, only dark waters and the occasional glimpse of light from a distant yacht, though that still added to the ambiance.

For starters, Nolan ordered a black truffle soup. I settled on a smoked salmon platter—no more pseudo-Cuban stuff, *gracias*! When a poised and friendly waiter brought the dishes to our table, Nolan asked for extra bread and joked about his carb intake.

"Carbs don't count when you're on vacation," the waiter quipped.

"Right you are! Bring me more butter too."

Another Buena Vista Social Club song played in the background. Was that the only Cuban music that the *Narwhal* people knew? This time it was Compay Segundo's "*De Camino a la Vereda*." In his smoky voice, he crooned, "Don't leave your way to take a road," admonishing a man who had dumped his girlfriend, Geraldina, for a less-deserving partner named Dorotea.

"It has been good to get away from Gainesville," Nolan said, taking my hand and kissing it.

He reminded me of his former self, the guy who would wine and dine me in Havana to win my heart.

"We both needed a break," I said.

"Sorry I have been so down. " He squeezed my fingers. "It has nothing to do with you. I just can't stand the idea of having to start over at nearly fifty. I've tried to 'reinvent' myself as a translator, but it's harder than I expected."

It broke my heart to hear that. He had always said that translations were too much work and paid next to nothing.

"You're a good professor, *papito*. And you didn't like those Point South types anyway. They didn't deserve you. You'll find a better job."

"Thank you, sweetheart." He was tearing up, back on full *llorón* mode again. "I really, really hated to let you down."

Let *me* down? If he thought his academic position mattered to me, he was sorely mistaken. I loved him for who he was, not what he did for a living.

"Maybe I could get a gig at the University of Havana," he added.

I laughed. "They'll pay you in pesos."

"But the cost of living is much cheaper there . . ." He shook his head and laughed too. "Just joking."

For entrées, we both ordered duck confit since it sounded oh-so-chic. It came with caramelized onions, sautéed potatoes and a fresh salad. Nolan chewed enthusiastically. He had recovered his appetite. Mine was back too, tempted by the sweet, crispy and tender duck meat. Fortunately, there were no sudden announcements over the loudspeakers to spoil the moment. Selfa must have been located, I concluded. I didn't need to keep worrying about her. Everything *was* fine.

"Did I tell you I have lined up three interviews at

the Modern Language Association's convention?" he asked after our dishes were empty and our bellies full.

He hadn't.

"That's terrific, *papito*." I leaned on his shoulder, feeling a surge of optimism. "Are they good schools?"

"One is, San Diego State. The two in the Midwest are so-so. But these are all tenure-track positions. I also got a call from a community college in Santa Barbara, though I'd rather wait and see what happens in January."

We had been in San Diego once for a conference, and I'd fallen in love with Balboa Park and SeaWorld. There was even a Cuban restaurant called Andrés.

Santa Barbara was probably just as nice. I would miss Miami and Candela, but you've gotta do what you've gotta do, right?

"You'll get an offer. Or more than one, and you can have your pick."

He kissed me on the cheek this time. His face smelled like aftershave and cologne. His eyes were clear and reflected the shine from the silver globes above us. I kissed him back, thinking again of the *viejitos* I'd seen at Maelstrom. Those two had probably weathered several storms as well.

A trip to the restroom led me to the discovery of a

small bar tucked in a corner. It had a polished wood counter and a strip of blue lights. The cocktail list featured my favorite, Peach Passion, with champagne and vodka, but I refrained from ordering. Starters, entrees and desserts were free, but booze wasn't. I finally understood the reason for the "onboard alcohol policy."

We finished off our meal with Baked Alaska and tiramisu.

Nolan hadn't heard from the elusive Doctor Fernández yet and he couldn't check his email because his phone didn't pick up a signal. We tried with mine, but it didn't work either. It had worked, however, while we were in the Miami port. I began to suspect that there was an "onboard Internet policy" as well.

The movie was about to start. Arm in arm, we walked to the theater. Only twenty or so of the red velvet chairs were occupied.

"I wonder why more people aren't interested in the cultural aspects of the cruise," Nolan mused.

The movie was *The Last Supper*, a 1976 flick by Tomás Gutiérrez Alea, who had been dead since 1996. The story line took place in the eighteenth century. The presenter, a sixty-something lady who spoke impeccable

Castilian-accented Spanish, described it as "a satire on slavery and colonialism."

"This is a masterpiece," she concluded.

It was a masterpiece all right. Fifteen minutes later, my eyelids got heavy. Soon the music, whip cracks and shouting from the screen faded into background. When Nolan patted my arm, waking me up, the credits were already rolling.

We stumbled together to our cabin. The narcotic effect of *The Last Supper* was still in full force because I fell asleep the minute my head hit the pillow.

4: Bienvenidos a La Habana

When I woke up the next morning at a quarter to nine, a new message flashed on the TV screen: *Bienvenidos a La Habana.*

I opened the balcony door and looked out. The *Narwhal* was docked in the Havana harbor. The Morro Castle with its old stone lighthouse stood to our right. The sky was clear and the sun shining. It felt good to be home again. Because, despite its many problems, Cuba was still home. *Mi casa, mi país.* It gave me a sense of security that had been conspicuously absent for the duration of the cruise.

Nolan, already dressed in his formal *el profesor*'s attire, was fumbling with his phone. Like the day before, there was no Internet signal.

"If Doctor Fernández has written to say he'll be waiting for us somewhere, I have no way of answering," he said, pacing the stateroom.

"Can you just call him?"

"I don't think I have his phone number. We've been communicating by email the whole time."

"You mean you don't *know* him?"

"Not personally."

"How did you get in touch with him?"

"I didn't. He was the one who wrote to me. He had read my book about Cuban socialist realism."

"Isn't his number somewhere in the emails?"

"Maybe, but since I can't access them—"

There was technology for you. One little doodah fails and everything messes up.

"I thought I had printed his invitation," Nolan added, emptying his suitcase on the armchair. "But I can't find that either."

"There are several free Wi-Fi hotspots in Havana," I told him. "One isn't far from Mamina's house. You can come with me, read your messages and arrange everything from there."

"Perfect!" He smiled, relieved. "So we'd go to your grandma's house first and then together to the lecture, right?"

I paused. I didn't exactly *enjoy* lectures. On socialist realism, *menos. Gracias, pero no.*

"Mamina expects me to stay home with her. But everyone can come have dinner with us later!"

"I don't want to impose on her."

"No worries. Mamina loves having people over. She'll be happy to cook for us."

Both statements were half-truths, if not total fabrications. Mamina didn't like to have guests, particularly if she didn't know them, and she would have rather spent the evening talking to me and not slaving away in the kitchen. But *I* would cook for them.

Somewhat soothed, Nolan suggested we have a light breakfast at Maelstrom—even though neither of us was hungry after last night's feast, but disembarkation would be underway by the time we returned to the cabin.

Cups of watery coffee in hand—espresso was considered a "specialty drink" for which you had to pay—we sat on the pool deck. Most passengers were ready to go ashore with straw hats, cameras and suntan lotions that smelled of almond and coconut oil. But the gangplank wasn't yet in place, and there was no sign that we would be getting off the boat anytime soon.

It was past nine-thirty when an announcement came over the PA system. We would be disembarking at 11 A.M., two hours after the scheduled time. A now-familiar tension rose in my chest. Would it be possible that they hadn't located Selfa yet? She couldn't still be missing, could she?

"Let's hope there isn't some last-minute issue," Nolan said. "It would be terrible if they turn the ship away because of a legal technicality."

He went back to the cabin while I headed down to guest services. The sense of doom had returned. With a vengeance. I had the gut-wrenching feeling that the problem wasn't a "legal technicality," but something much worse.

THE GUEST SERVICES AREA was a beehive. People were having their pictures taken by the onboard photographer against a background of fake palm trees and nagging the clerks about the schedule change. A few purchased last-minute excursions not included in the cruise package. There were only three offers: a short guided tour of the Morro Castle, one of Cathedral Square and a visit to Hemingway Museum at Finca La Vigía that included lunch and was supposed to take most of the afternoon—"only" ninety dollars per person.

I was making my way to the information desk when I felt it again: the stare. The same one from the day before while I'd been looking for the library. I pretended to examine a Varadero Beach poster and peered around. I saw nothing suspicious. Behind me were two women repeating phrases in Spanish. To my right, a middle-aged couple wanted to arrange an *almendrón* ride for that evening.

"We aren't allowed to deal directly with locals," the guest service clerk said. "I'm sorry, but you'd have to do that on your own."

The skinny guy who resembled a hippie, still in his tie-dyed shirt, sprinted past me toward the smoking area with a fat cigar in hand. Other eager smokers followed.

The old man with the gold chains was around too. This time he sported a Grateful Dead cap. He leered hungrily at a pretty girl in a sarong. He might have been the one watching me. *Viejo cochino.*

He walked to the "Shore Excursions" desk and asked in faltering English what time he was supposed to be back that evening.

"Anytime you want, sir," answered a woman in a starched white uniform, "because we're going to spend the night docked in Havana. We aren't leaving for Nassau until tomorrow at six P.M., though the passengers need to be there by three."

"I know that, *mija*, but I don't want you guys to start worrying if I don't show up tonight."

The woman, who didn't seem to like being *mija*ed,

sighed a little too loudly and said, "We take our guests' safety seriously, sir. Just note that if you're not on board by eleven o'clock tonight, you'll miss the Perseids."

My heart thudded. I got closer so as not to miss a word of the conversation.

"What's that?" Grateful Dead asked.

"A meteor shower that will peak this evening, sir. We'll leave the harbor for two hours so our guests can enjoy it away from the city lights. It's truly spectacular!"

Grateful Dead didn't seem interested. He soon sauntered away.

"Do you have any more information about that meteor shower?" I asked the clerk.

She handed me a printed page.

"Here is a write-up with all the details, madam."

ENJOY THE BEST CELESTIAL SHOW OF THE YEAR ABOARD THE *NARWHAL*!

Don't miss one of the most remarkable sightings of this tour. Tonight, the popular Perseid meteor shower will be visible from about 9 P.M. through dawn, the peak being between 11 P.M. and 3 A.M.

We'll leave port between 11 P.M. and 1 A.M. to be beyond the reach of land-based light pollution.

Onboard astronomer Mark Trujillo will lead the meteor-watching session and answer questions. Binoculars will be provided.

5: Bacuranao Beach

That tonight was the Perseid meteor shower *couldn't* be a coincidence. I folded the page as anxiety rose inside my chest. I found a leather couch, sat down and closed my eyes, and there it was again—the past, looking straight at me. The night I had (kind of) seen the meteor shower. The dark sky, clouds pregnant with rain, the salty ocean smell. And Lorenzo's big disappointment.

IT WAS ONLY A few months into our relationship when he asked me to go with him to Bacuranao Beach at night. The reason was to watch the season's "celestial event."

"Why can't we watch it from your balcony or my rooftop?" I had asked.

"Because of light pollution, Merceditas. It washes out everything. And I want you to take a good look at the Perseids. There will be up to forty meteors per hour!"

Lorenzo didn't know how much I hated *Las Perseidas*. Not the meteor shower, but its namesake book, with which he spent way too much time. Time he could have been spending with *me*. He had a laptop, a gift from Kiel, and would sit for hours in front of it, "fine-tuning the story," he said, even when I was at the apartment. I was so jealous of the novel that I'd discarded the pages he sometimes showed me. Not that they were easy to read, either. He printed them at the Faculty with a dot-matrix printer that never had enough ink.

But I'd agreed to go to the beach because the trip sounded exciting. More so after Lorenzo had borrowed a motorcycle to take us there, and most importantly, bring us back to the city—the meteor peak would happen around one in the morning, and buses stopped circulating after midnight. That was my first time on a Harley (a very old one, but still), and I drank it all up: the wind on my face, my hair floating behind me, my arms hugging Lorenzo's strong back. Neither of us wore helmets; they were unheard of in Cuba back then.

We had arrived at Bacuranao at eleven o'clock. Lorenzo had brought a small telescope. The beach, about three blocks from the closest houses, looked oddly quiet. There had been an empty kiosk where beer and sandwiches were sold during the day, and Lorenzo secured the motorcycle under the awning. Then he placed a couple of towels on the sand, mounted the telescope and waited for the meteors to make a grand entrance in the Bacuranao sky.

"The only thing that worries me is those clouds up north," he had said. "I hope they don't spoil the view."

I couldn't keep my eyes off him. His angular face and shoulder-length hair made him look like a hero from times past. A knight, perhaps. We had just watched *King Arthur*, though Lorenzo hadn't liked it because of historical inaccuracies.

At first, I had thought the outing would turn into a romantic escapade. I had even imagined that the meteor shower was an excuse to make out, and perhaps more, under the stars. My twenty-year-old hormones were anticipating a feast, but Lorenzo, though usually a passionate lover, wasn't in the mood for that. Instead, he chose the moment to give a lecture on . . . writers and books.

"I've always been partial to French authors. Not necessarily the classics, though of course I love Flaubert and Zola—they were true masters. But I'm more drawn to the adventure and genre writers, like Jules Verne and Alexandre Dumas."

Then Lorenzo had veered out into his own path

as a writer. How it had come to pass that after many years of reading and analyzing other people's novels, he realized he could write one as well.

"I already knew the techniques and only had to apply them. The problem is time, Merceditas. It has taken me years to complete my first novel, and it isn't ready yet. But I'm close to finishing—ah, when *Las Perseidas* is finally published, I will have a signing at the book fair in La Cabaña. I'll make sure that my students and everybody I know get a copy of it."

I had never been to a book fair and didn't have a clear idea of what people did there. But I didn't want to interrupt him with questions or be called *burra* again. Besides, I understood that this mattered a lot to Lorenzo. Those were his dreams. Not Macarena dreams like mine, but important, grown-up aspirations. I was proud that he trusted me with them. I inhaled the pungent smell of the ocean and caressed my boyfriend's hair as he talked away.

His book, he had said, was a space opera, a statement that didn't make a lot of sense to me. The only operas I had heard of were those staged at the National Theater, to which, of course, I had never been either.

"So is it about the meteor shower and the stuff that happens out there in space?" I had asked timidly.

"Yes, but that setting is just a metaphor. When you look up, *mi amor*"—he pointed at the sky—"you are actually looking back across the immensity of time. Think of the light of those stars traveling hundreds, even thousands of years before they reach us."

A small fireball streaked across the sky.

"Look, Merceditas! That's the first one. There will be so many more!"

I watched and had done my best to look impressed, but the meteor shower wasn't the magnificent light show Lorenzo had made it out to be. It was more like third-class firecrackers.

We kept staring up, but soon the clouds had taken over. A few minutes before midnight, a downpour hit. We got soaked.

Lorenzo dragged the telescope under the kiosk awning, which smelled like motorcycle oil, and let out a disappointed sigh.

"We'll have to wait until next year. For now, we have been cheated out of the Perseids."

CHEATED OUT OF THE Perseids.

I opened my eyes. I was still sitting on the leather couch surrounded by people running around, the phone photography flashes and *"El Cuarto de Tula"* playing in the background. Was it my imagination or did the "Shore Excursion" operator look concerned? Ditto for the other clerk. Were they all worried about Selfa? Had "Mr. Ostargó" shown up for the muster drill after all? I could ask but didn't trust my voice. Besides, they might demand to know why I was so interested in them. I didn't want to come off as paranoid or unhinged.

A clock over the guest service desk read ten-fifteen. Maybe too early, but I needed a drink.

6: Doctor Fernández's Message

Ned Land's Bar was just a few feet away. I ordered a glass of Merlot and distracted myself by looking at paintings of giant whales and sharks that hung from the walls among fishing nets and harpoons.

Grateful Dead trailed in five minutes later and asked for a shot of rum.

"With Havana Club Siete Años," he told the bartender in Spanish. Cuban-sounding Spanish.

How many of us were there on this ship? Though he could have been Puerto Rican or Dominican, their accent being similar to ours. I almost wanted to ask if he'd gotten a free ticket too. But that would have seemed intrusive. Instead, to take my mind off *Las Perseidas*, The Viking and Selfa's disappearance, I quizzed the bartender about the pink cocktail with condensed milk.

"Ah, that's *medias de seda*. Grenadine, rum, cinnamon and, yes, condensed milk. Would you like one?"

"Sure."

I had chugged down my wine but still felt out of sorts. Those damn meteors . . . Another drink would help.

Then Technophobe Tim came in. I recognized his salt-and-pepper goatee and slicked-back hair. He wasn't with the tired-looking blonde I'd met the day before. A younger woman in a flowery, flimsy dress was by his side this time. He didn't notice my presence, and they sat with their backs to me. I listened—without intending, as usual—to the chat between him and his companion.

"So we're all here to have fun, that's what I think," he said.

"And what is fun for you?"

Grateful Dead watched, amused, as the bartender made the *medias de seda*. When offered one, he chuckled.

"*No, chico, no, eso no sirve pa na*. Bring me another shot of rum."

Definitely Cuban. The way he'd said "not worth the trouble" gave him away.

"You know that saying 'what happens in Vegas'?" the goatee guy was purring. "Well, the same applies here, eh? What happens on a cruise ship—"

The *medias de seda* didn't disappoint. It tasted, now that I took the time to evaluate it, like an adult milkshake. I gave the bartender my onboard card and signed the twenty-dollar receipt, hoping Nolan wouldn't look at the final bill too closely.

Grateful Dead was getting sloshed. Next-door Tim and his new lady laughed and not-so-discreetly pawed each other. I headed back to the cabin, waiting for the alcohol to kick in before I gave any more thought to the meteor shower. I couldn't deal with it just yet.

THE CONTENTS OF NOLAN'S suitcase were still spread out on the armchair. I brushed my teeth and carefully washed my mouth so he couldn't detect the smell of alcohol.

"Doctor Fernández hasn't emailed me yet, but I found the invitation," he said, waving it as I came out of the bathroom with my most innocent expression. "And there's a phone number too!"

"Phew."

While he placed the call, I plopped down on my sofa bed, picked up the printed message and looked at it without much interest at first.

From: lfernandez2323@gmail.com
To: nspivey@pointsouth.edu
Dear Dr. Spivey,

I am pleased to extend an invitation to you to be

a visiting scholar at the University of Havana's Faculty of Arts and Letters. You have been selected because your research in the field of socialist realism is of great interest to us and relevant to the mission of our Literature Department.

As proposed, you will deliver a lecture about the life and works of renowned Cuban writer Manuel Cofiño and his contributions to contemporary Caribbean literature. Additionally, we expect that you will be involved in an evening educational event attended by faculty, staff and students.

You are responsible for adhering to all proper immigration procedures of the Republic of Cuba.

We look forward to your time at the University of Havana. We believe that our students will benefit from your lecture and presence, and that this cultural exchange will allow us to learn much from each other.

Revolutionarily,
L. N. Fernández, PhD
Caribbean Literature Professor
Facultad de Artes y Letras de La Habana
8787644

My skin rippled in goosebumps. Nolan had never mentioned that his lecture was going to be delivered at my (and Lorenzo's) old stomping grounds. He had just talked about the University of Havana in a general way. Though there was nothing odd about it. Nolan used to take his FIU students to the Faculty of Arts and Letters for summer courses, so it made sense that they had invited him.

"Doctor Fernández isn't answering." He tossed the phone on his sofa bed with more force than necessary.

"If that's his office number, he won't be there. Today's Sunday."

"Shit!"

He wasn't the type to ever curse. He must be *really* stressed. I reread the message and noticed the sender's email address.

"Has Doctor Fernández always written to you from this email account?" I asked.

"I think so. Why?"

"In Cuba, uh.cu is the domain for all higher ed institutions, the equivalent of .edu. The professors' email addresses end in uh.cu too. Why is he using Gmail?"

Nolan glanced at the TV screen, where a new announcement was posted. Disembarkation had been delayed "until further notice."

"Aren't government-run servers unreliable in Cuba, Mercy?"

"They are. But sending an official invitation to a foreign colleague from a personal account isn't appropriate. You know *that*."

He shrugged. "What's the big deal?"

I tried to remember if there had been a Doctor Fernández among my professors. Of course, that had been nine years ago.

"What's this guy's first name?"

"I'm not sure, Mercy. I think it's Luis."

"You *think*?"

A second muster drill was called.

"They haven't found Selfa yet," I blurted out. "This must be about her too."

"Selfa who?"

"That woman they've been calling. She's been missing since yesterday."

Nolan paused, a cleft forming between his eyebrows.

I was ready to tell him about meeting her and Javier the day before and the uncanny coincidences that were making my stomach turn. But a more urgent call to gather in our muster stations came.

7: Open Bar

Back in the library, in front of the Bahamas nautical chart, Alicia did her best to answer questions from a gaggle of passengers fighting for her attention. They all looked, and sounded, mad.

"How long are we going to be kept on board?" a man asked. "We only get a full day in Havana, and it's being wasted!"

"We're very sorry for the inconvenience, sir," Alicia said.

"Sorry won't cut it. Let us out of here!"

Others joined in.

"This is ridiculous."

"I want a refund!" a woman shrieked. "I didn't pay over five thousand dollars to be kept hostage on a ship!"

Alicia apologized again. I wanted to tell the grumblers to shut up or go talk to the captain. It wasn't the crew's fault.

I stepped outside. Several burly guys in plainclothes

but looking very much like security walked up and down the halls.

The drill turned out to be just a head count and was over in less than five minutes.

"People are so rude!" I told Alicia. "You shouldn't have to put up with it."

She pursed her lips. "Thanks. But that was nothing. I've heard much worse, believe me."

"Is this all about Selfa?"

She didn't answer. I realized crewmembers weren't allowed to discuss such issues with passengers.

"*¿Hablas español*, Alicia*?*"

"*¡Sí!* I'm Puerto Rican."

"I'm Cuban."

"*Chévere.*"

The whiner who had asked for a refund was having a meltdown. Alicia hurried over to soothe her. I stayed in the library, thinking of the Perseid meteor shower and Lorenzo's book. The free cruise, Javier, Selfa, Kiel, Doctor Fernández's Gmail address . . . I remembered the Nautilus representative, the poodle jumping from the grooming table. It only occurred to me now that the rep had not asked me my name. She had known who I was and what I looked like when she walked into the store . . .

When Alicia came back shaking her head in frustration, I asked her, "Did Nautilus offer many giveaway tickets for this cruise?"

"We always have last-minute deals like beverage and dining packages and some half-priced excursions."

"No, I mean free tickets."

"Tickets, for free?" She chuckled. "No way, *mi hermana*. Not for Cuba, much less this time of the year."

So that was it. Someone had paid for our trip. And Selfa's, and maybe Javier's as well.

Nolan came over, cellphone dangling from his hand. Alicia explained that the phone's Internet wouldn't work on board.

"Not even with data?"

"No, but we have Wi-Fi packages, sir. Forty dollars for an hour or one hundred for three hours. And you can use the onboard computers if you want."

"Geez, that's a lot of money," Nolan groaned. "I only need to check my messages. It won't take more than five minutes."

"I'll see about getting you a discount." She winked at me. "The *Caribeña* special."

"*¡Gracias!*"

She led us to the business center. In the meantime, an overly cheerful voice from the loudspeakers announced that "all guests would be provided with complimentary drinks to compensate for the delay." I left Nolan parked in front of a computer and joined the stampede for the open bar. It wasn't just the free booze, though that wouldn't hurt. I needed time alone to process everything I'd just found out.

The Devilfish was better avoided because most people already knew about it and would go straight to deck twelve. Ned Land's was too small and would become crowded quickly. I returned to the bar inside Nemo's Table, which was still almost empty, and ordered a margarita.

The bartender moistened the glass rim with a lemon wedge before dipping it into a bowl filled with salt crystals. The rim sparkled under the blue lights. I watched as the guy mixed tequila reposado, Cointreau and lime juice in the cocktail shaker, added ice and swirled. But I missed the last part of the ceremony—straining the cocktail into the margarita glass—because someone slid onto the barstool next to me.

"*¡Coño!*" I jumped.

"Sorry, Merceditas," Javier said. "I didn't mean to startle you."

"It's okay. I was just thinking."

"I've been thinking too."

Three couples showed up, followed by a party of five. Javier asked for a glass of Cabernet Sauvignon. After being elbowed and pushed by the newcomers, he suggested we sit at a nearby table. I licked the salt beads on the glass rim and took a sip. Ah, the tang of lime and tequila melting in the bittersweetness of Cointreau! Shouldn't clash too much with the *medias de seda* and the Merlot from earlier.

"Where's your husband?" Javier asked.

"Checking his email."

He took a long swallow of wine.

"You know the Casa deal I told you about? They haven't *technically* offered for me to teach the writing workshop yet. It was mentioned as a possibility, but everything was . . . vague."

Exactly what Nolan had said about his exchange with Doctor Fernández. I started drinking my margarita faster than I'd intended.

"My English isn't good enough to write for American magazines, but—"

Could it be possible that Javier hadn't actually met any of those Casa people either? I cut him off in midsentence. "Who paid for your trip?"

He shifted in his chair. "A woman named Yordanka. I believe she's a Casa employee. Why?"

"Have you spoken to her?"

"No. The whole exchange was done by email."

"Does she have a Casa de las Américas email address?"

"I don't remember—didn't pay attention to that. Why does it matter?"

I finished the margarita and stared at the empty glass.

Javier went on, "I am now, like they say here, on the skinny branches of the tree. *Vamos, más pobre que puta en Cuaresma.* No matter what happens with Casa, I need to find a job, any job, soon. Would it be possible to ask your husband . . . What's his name, eh?"

"Nolan."

"Would it be possible for Nolan to get me a teaching gig at the college where he works? It can be anything—a creative writing class, a journalism workshop, whatever, as long as it's in Spanish. They won't hire me as a full-time professor or even an adjunct because I don't have a green card, but I can work as a visiting writer if an insider recommends me. Do you think he might be able to help?"

Not at all, but that was beside the point now.

"Listen. The guy who invited Nolan contacted him through email, just like this Casa woman did you," I said.

"Everything's done online these days."

"Then there's Selfa. The professor I told you about yesterday? She won the same 'free trip' my husband

and I did. But I just asked an employee, and the free trips don't exist."

He gave me a half-shrug. "What are you talking about, Merceditas?"

"Selfa wrote the book that Lorenzo gave you to read, the novel you rejected. She was jealous and some people thought she was the one that accused him of writing a counterrevolutionary novel."

"She did?" He sounded surprised.

"Yes! That's how Lorenzo ended up in prison."

Javier narrowed his eyes. "But what does that have to do with . . . ?"

And *I* was the one that people called *burra*.

"We all had something to do with Lorenzo at one time or another," I explained slowly. "You stole his book. I cheated on him with Nolan. Selfa filed false charges against him. But there's more." I lowered my voice. "I think Kiel's here too."

"Kiel who?"

The bartender came to our table with a tray of margaritas. I grabbed one and Javier another. We started drinking at the same time.

"The Viking. Lorenzo's Danish friend."

His face went pale.

"Are you sure?"

"Well, I haven't seen him, but I did hear his name during the drill."

"I don't understand what you are getting at, Merceditas." He wiped sweat from his brow though the air in the restaurant was cool.

"Someone has brought all of us here."

"All of us?" he echoed.

"You, Nolan, Selfa and me. And that someone could very well be Kiel."

There it was. The thought that had been on the back of my mind since the day before, creeping up despite my attempts to ignore it.

Javier didn't answer right away. I couldn't read his expression. Surprise? Fear? The bar was too dim to tell.

"But why would he do that?" he muttered at last.

"Why do you think? To throw a party in our honor?"

Again, it took him a while to process the idea, or to pretend he was processing it.

"That's silly, Merceditas."

"It isn't. Kiel and Lorenzo were best friends. Like brothers!"

Javier drank furiously. I watched him—his rodent-like countenance, with furtive eyes and a small mouth. When he spoke again, his voice was shaky wand hoarse.

"I have always suspected that Lorenzo was killed."

8: The Fight

Javier's words didn't shock me as much as they should have. I had never believed the suicide or the accident stories.

The bartender brought more margaritas to our table. "These are rimmed with sugar," he announced.

They could've been rimmed with cat litter for all I cared. Though my head was buzzing, I drank desperately anyway until I gathered the courage to ask Javier, "What makes you think so?"

"I saw it happen."

I choked on the margarita. "You did!"

"Well, no," he backtracked. "Not with my own eyes. But—"

Javier's face turned ashen under the silver globes. He spoke in a low tone, not looking at me.

"I hadn't heard from Lorenzo in about three weeks when news of his imprisonment reached Barcelona. A friend told me he had been accused of writing a subversive book. I immediately flew to Havana, went to Villa Marista and, after much pleading, met with a Seguridad agent. I had brought in a copy of *Las Perseidas*, hoping it would help to exonerate Lorenzo. As you remember, the book was a fantasy novel where the words 'Cuba' and 'revolution' didn't even appear.

"Not long after that, a different Seguridad agent paid me a surprise visit at the Tryp Habana Libre, where I was staying. He returned the manuscript and said that Lorenzo was only a person of interest in an ongoing investigation. 'The revolution appreciates his commitment to education,' he said and left me with the impression that the problem wasn't too serious. The Cuban political police were overzealous, but that was that."

"*Overzealous*, Javier?" I couldn't help but say. "That's a mild way of putting it."

He leaned earnestly toward me.

"What I mean is, Lorenzo didn't need me. The plane ticket and the hotel stay had been a waste of time and money, I thought. Indeed, a few days later, Lorenzo was free. He called me and said it all had been a mistake. He also hinted that his Danish friend was 'connected' and had been instrumental in setting him free. The Faculty dean and some of his colleagues had been supportive too. He was going to get his job back and settle a score with whoever had slandered him. He might have mentioned Selfa at that point, but I honestly don't remember. What I *do* remember is how much he missed you. 'Merceditas's the woman of my life,' he said. 'I hope she's happy now, but I don't know how I'm going to live without her.'"

"Did he really say that?" I asked, anguished.

"I swear he did." Javier wiped his brow. "The whole thing came as a surprise because I didn't even know you guys had broken up. Last time Lorenzo and I had seen each other was a few months back, when the Dane had taken all of us to celebrate the fact that the book was a finalist, remember?"

I nodded sadly, flashing back to El Floridita and our meal of lobster and hope.

"Then one of the Saint Jordi judges—the owner of the publishing house that sponsored the contest and had initially shown interest in the novel—emailed me. Since I was representing Lorenzo, I had sent the manuscript from my email account, but under his name, of course. The publisher, who knew me because everybody knows everybody in Barcelona's literary world, asked if I had used a nom de plume. The manuscript had made it to the last round and was going to be either the winner or the runner-up. In his opinion, it deserved first place, but he wanted to find out who the author was.

"The judges were hesitant because it's a crapshoot to publish an unknown writer, and even more so one living in another country. But I wouldn't have lied or stolen the book from Lorenzo. In fact, I called him right away to discuss a promotional strategy: we could market him as a courageous Cuban intellectual, recently imprisoned by the political police because of his work. It would garner him interviews in Spain and help sell the book. The publisher might even pay for his ticket to Barcelona and help him get settled there. But Lorenzo refused. He wasn't obsessed with leaving the island, like so many Cubans I knew."

I drank the last of my sweet margarita. Yes, Lorenzo could have asked for political asylum in Paris or New York, as many of his colleagues had done after attending conferences there. "Why should I?" he had always said. "This is my country." That was one of the reasons I gave myself for dropping him. Not that I was "obsessed" with leaving, but I'd of course toyed with the idea, even before meeting Nolan.

"We agreed on getting together that evening before I got back to the publisher," Javier went on. "We hadn't yet had a chance to meet after his release. Around seven o'clock, I knocked on his door. Nobody answered, but I heard angry voices inside. Lorenzo was calling someone *hijoeputa* and *cabrón*, and whoever was with him replied with a mix of Spanish and foreign words. There was a thump, a loud gasp and more cursing. I figured that he was arguing with the Dane and decided not to get involved. He and Lorenzo were big, tall guys, and I had no desire to play referee—"

"How did you know it was Kiel?"

Javier rubbed the end of his nose.

"Because he had an accent. And he was the only foreigner Lorenzo was friends with."

"Not the *only* foreigner," I replied. "He knew others from those academic events he went to. That's how he and Nolan met."

"Your husband?" Javier gave me a sideways glance. "Was he in Havana then?"

"No, he was in Miami with me."

Or not? I remembered that conference he had attended a few weeks after I had come from Cuba. But I wasn't too sure about the dates. Besides, Nolan wouldn't—I fidgeted with my empty margarita glass and asked, "So what else happened?"

"I left and had a beer at El Paladar de Carmela while

waiting for the dust to settle. Carmela always liked to chat with me about Spain, but she was in a hurry because there was going to be a blackout that night. We didn't talk much. I went back to the building at a quarter to eight.

"The smell hit me in the stairs, the unmistakable, thick stench of burned wood. A woman and three kids rushed out. 'There's a fire!' the woman yelled, pushing me out of their way. I kept expecting to see Lorenzo and the other guy come out, but they didn't. The firemen arrived. After they doused the flames, Lorenzo's body was taken out in the stretcher. He—" Javier stopped, his hands over his face, sobbing quietly.

A blast of horror and anger rose through my chest.

"Why . . . why the hell didn't you go to the police and report it?" My words came out garbled. The margaritas, the *medias de seda* and the wine were finally catching up to me.

Javier composed himself and blew his nose.

"I was afraid, Merceditas. That Danish bastard had friends in high places. As easily as he had helped free Lorenzo, he could have thrown me in jail. Lorenzo was dead, anyway. There was nothing to do."

"Except steal his book."

"It wasn't like that!" he answered defensively. "I

didn't plan it. But back in Barcelona the publisher insisted, asking again if I had written *Las Perseidas*. He thought I had used a pen name because my first book hadn't done well, so the judges wouldn't be prejudiced against the new one. I finally said yes."

I felt the urge to strangle him.

"Nobody in Spain had heard of Lorenzo Alvear." He raised his shoulders. "I was taking a chance, but the novel would never be sold in Cuba. Lorenzo hadn't shown the manuscript to many people. One or two colleagues and you, he said. I told the publisher to change the title and—"

"Mercy!"

Nolan was in front of us.

"*¿Qué pasa?*"

"I've been looking for you all over the ship!"

"You the professor?" Javier slurred.

I stood up and struggled to keep my balance. Nolan's jaw dropped.

"For God's sake, Mercy!"

9: "You're Still in Love with Him"

Next thing I knew, Nolan and I were back in the cabin, and he was splashing my face with cold water from the crystal carafe.

"Hey, *comemierda*, stop it!" I pushed him away.

The mirror over the dresser showed me a pitiful image—pale lips and cheeks, reddish eyes—so different from the happy, playful woman I had seen the day before. My hair looked electrified. I threw myself on the recently made sofa bed and turned toward the wall. Nolan's voice rang in my ears for a few minutes until an alcohol-soaked cloud drowned it.

THE LIGHT THAT CAME from the balcony hurt my eyes. My skull throbbed. I wanted to throw up. The TV clock read twelve forty-five.

Without saying a word, Nolan brought me a cup of coffee. I took a sip, wondering why he looked so pissed off.

"You have a drinking problem," he stated, more serious than I had ever seen him. "Mercy, you need to go get help."

His words sounded like running water. What was his problem? Nobody had ever called me a *borracha* in Cuba. Lorenzo certainly never had.

Lorenzo! Javier's story came back to me all at once, along with my fears and guilt. The Viking had murdered Lorenzo. He might be after us now—he was on board the ship.

"We'll be disembarking at two o'clock." Nolan pointed to the screen where a new announcement had appeared. "You can stay with your grandmother, rest for a few hours and, hopefully, be sober enough to cook dinner when we finish the event at the Faculty. *If* you still want to do that. If you don't, please say so before you embarrass me in front of Doctor Fernández."

"That man doesn't exist," I said.

He startled a little. "What do you mean?"

"It's a trap! We've been led here. There's no Doctor Fernández, no free tickets, no nothing."

"Mercy, you're not well. Listen—"

"No, *you* listen to *me*!"

I blundered through the story, from my early encounter with Selfa to Kiel's name being called out to Javier's revelations. There was no way to bypass Lorenzo, so I ended up talking about him, maybe too much, only to realize at the sight of Nolan's hardened face that it had been a mistake.

He took his time to reply. When he finally did, he spat, "You're still in love with him."

It was my turn to keep silent.

He sank down on his sofa bed, facing me. There was a bitterness in his voice that I had never heard before.

"I knew it, and that was why I didn't want to marry you at first. But I did, hoping you'd eventually forget Lorenzo. I was wrong. You think about him all the time. His ghost follows us everywhere. He lives with us. He sleeps in our bed. He's even here."

"This isn't about me being in love with Lorenzo, which is ridiculous." My face was burning but I tried to remain cool. "It's about the people who betrayed him: Selfa, Javier, you and, yes, myself. And Kiel," I added, though I didn't know anymore how The Viking fit into the equation.

Nolan straightened.

"*I* didn't betray Lorenzo!" he yelled. "*You* left him for me. Because you loved me—or so you said."

"You don't get it, do you? Javier told—"

"Stop it!" He raised his hand.

I wasn't sure if he just wanted me to shut up or was ready to hit me. We'd never had a physical fight, and he wasn't a violent man, but the anger in his eyes frightened me. Just in case, I shut up.

A long, painful pause followed. I avoided my husband's eyes, wanting to kick myself. *En boca cerrada no entran moscas*, Mamina used to say. I had opened my big yap and now had to swallow the flies.

Fortunately, when Nolan spoke again, he was back to his usual, kind self.

"Sorry I got so upset, Mercy. But when you start drinking like that, I fear I'm losing you. The woman I love goes away. And then, all this talk about Lorenzo . . . You were right. Hard as it is to admit, it *was* a betrayal. I've always felt bad about the way I handled it."

I felt tears welling up and looked out, focusing on the view of the Morro Castle against the deep-blue sky.

"It was my fault too."

"You were too young and inexperienced. *I* should have talked to him." He sighed and rubbed the bridge of his nose. "But this guy's claims make no sense. First, you don't even know that he's telling the truth. I certainly wouldn't trust him. Didn't he steal Lorenzo's novel? And why would the rich Danish guy kill Lorenzo after helping him get out of prison?"

There was a possible answer to his question, but not one I felt like sharing with him. Not at that moment, anyway.

"Even if everything Javier said was true, why does it make you think that Doctor Fernández doesn't exist?"

Too fuzzy-brained to answer coherently, I just ignored the question.

"What about the tickets?" I asked. "Alicia told me that Nautilus didn't give any away."

"Who's Alicia?"

"The girl who led the muster drill."

"Mercy, that woman is a low-level crewmember. She doesn't have anything to do with the marketing department."

"You think I'm making this up?"

"I think you've overreacted. We have been going through a lot. Meeting these two . . . ghosts from the past"—he smiled in an obvious, painful effort to lighten the mood—"hasn't helped. But there's no reason to fear. The *Narwhal* has onboard security staff, didn't you see them this morning? And we are already in Cuba. This is a safe country."

"I know." I stood up. "I'm sorry. It was stupid of me to drink like that."

He watched, concerned, as I walked toward the door.

"I'm going to breathe in fresh air," I said. I paused briefly and faced him. "And by the way, I *do* love you. I hope you know it by now. I don't care for . . . anybody else."

He cupped my face and kissed me.

"I know, Mercy. I didn't mean that. I was just angry. Do you want me to go with you?"

I offered him a small, apologetic smile.

"I'd rather be alone, *papito*. I won't drink again, promise. Honestly, my body can't handle another drop of alcohol."

"Come back soon."

I nodded and slunk away.

10: Semi Affair at the Comodoro

Once outside the stateroom I leaned against the wall, feeling dizzy again. It wasn't just the booze, but the realization that Javier might be a liar. After all, he was a writer—a bad one, by his own admission. Writers are prone to lying, or at least exaggerating. There was no reason to believe that The Viking had killed Lorenzo and then set the place on fire. Though Javier hadn't said that outright. He had *implied* it, letting me jump to the conclusion myself.

I stumbled around looking for the elevators because I didn't trust my feet to navigate the velvet-carpeted stairs. It seemed like I was going in the wrong direction, as usual. I turned the other way, and another memory assaulted me. The Viking. Our senseless affair, or semi-affair. And the regret that followed.

IT WAS 2007, EARLY February. Up to then, I had been faithful to Lorenzo. Which wasn't difficult because guys my age didn't appeal to me anymore. Nolan was still a distant, polite American professor I had only seen a few times. I was happy with my boyfriend and the future we were planning together—getting married, living together in Villa Santa Marta, renting his place, having kids at some point . . .

That day, Lorenzo had gone to a faculty meeting. I was alone in the apartment when someone knocked on the door. Since there was no phone in the building, visitors just showed up unannounced, so it didn't surprise me to see Kiel there. But it felt a bit awkward. Though I'd known him for as long as I had been Lorenzo's girlfriend, we had only ever exchanged a few pleasantries.

He came in, and I apologized for not offering the customary cup of coffee. Lorenzo had still been waiting for his ration-card allocation.

"Oh, I'll bring him some next time."

His well-intentioned comment had irritated me. Our everyday life had been constantly plagued by shortages, but foreigners could buy anything they wanted. Of course, they had dollars. We didn't. But they were in *our* country. It wasn't fair.

Kiel sat down in a rocking chair without taking off the coat he kept on even during the hottest days.

I made an effort to play hostess. We started talking. Suddenly he was telling me about his childhood. He had been an athletic, outdoorsy kid growing up in a small town called Mariager.

"We have the longest and most beautiful fjord in Denmark. I loved it and never wanted to move to Chicago. I remember arguing with my dad. It was as if I knew that something bad was going to happen there."

"Have you been back to Denmark?"

"Yes, my relatives are still in Mariager. Good people, but we don't get along. At first, they wouldn't even want to talk about what I had gone through. Now they feel sorry for me, and I can't stand it. I'd rather be by myself, though that's hard too."

In turn, I told him about my mother, a topic that seldom surfaced in my conversations, even with Lorenzo. But Kiel's frankness, the vulnerability he had shown, made me open up.

"So she left? And your father's dead? Then you're an orphan, like Lorenzo and me."

He was right, though I'd never felt like one. Mamina was my mother, for all practical purposes.

"Have you ever thought about looking for your mom?" he'd asked.

"I can't even leave Cuba without an exit permit. And how would I pay for a plane ticket?"

A shadow of sadness crossed Kiel's face. He had looked kind and almost handsome despite the scars and discolored skin.

"If someone were to help . . ." he half offered.

"I don't know that I'd care to find her after all these years," I had lied, but the possibility had been left hanging between us like a piñata only slightly out of reach.

Having felt uneasy, though not sure about what, I asked about his upcoming trips.

"I'm going to spend two or three weeks in Granada, then head north to Santiago de Compostela. Someday I'll walk the Camino de Santiago, but would prefer not to do it alone. It's not fun to travel solo."

"Is that right?" I used to think that if you *could* travel it didn't matter with whom, or even where.

"Yes. It always feels like everyone but you is part of a group. Chatty friends, happy families—and me. It gets downright depressing."

Afterward Kiel had launched into a long tale about El Camino de Santiago, which he called "The Way." Soon, the notion of a spiritual journey piqued my interest. Going to Spain (or any foreign country, for that matter) would certainly "transform" me. Oh, to get out of Cuba, to see different cities, different people, different stores that sold different shoes! Despite Kiel's accent, or maybe because of it, his voice sounded like liquid silk. I listened, fascinated, feeling a mix of curiosity and wonder that slowly morphed into sexual attraction.

It was the Macarena effect.

Before, the poor guy had looked ugly as sin to me. He walked with a limp. The left side of his face was a sickly shade of pink, and a large scar crossed his cheek. He wore that frayed wig. But that day, I saw a new light in his silver-gray eyes. He had perfect white teeth. He was tall, like Lorenzo, and probably strong too. He *could* have been handsome.

He was also a good person, generous to a fault. Hadn't he paid for Lorenzo's ticket to the last MLA convention? Hadn't he constantly brought food and gifts for everyone? And a man like that was lonely and depressed? He needed a globe-trotting companion, didn't he? And the companion could be . . . well, me. But there was more. We could hire a private detective (my idea of private detectives at that time was shaped by the *Sherlock Holmes* reruns that Cuban TV unearthed from time to time) to find my mother.

All this had gone through my mind in a matter of seconds, blinding me to the implications of such plans for Lorenzo, Mamina, even myself.

I turned on Kiel what I hoped was my most dazzling, seductive smile. I moved my shoulders a certain way that never failed to get men's attention. It took a while, but he noticed and blushed. The air had changed between us, becoming intense and sticky.

It all happened so fast. We kissed and made out a little. I had thought of sneaking to the attic, but Lorenzo could've come in at any minute, and our presence upstairs would have been hard to explain.

After some hesitation, Kiel had shyly invited me to the Comodoro Hotel, where he was staying in a bungalow. *Casas particulares* were already gaining popularity among foreign tourists, but he didn't like them. A lack of privacy, he complained. Nosy owners. Neighbors who stared at him or tried to sell him junk. In government-run establishments, nobody cared about the guests, for better or for worse.

As he hailed a taxi on Paseo del Prado, I thought of Catalina's daughter, who had hooked up with that Spaniard and now had a beautiful home in Galicia. She wasn't the only one. So many girls my age had married foreigners and moved to Canada, Italy, Sweden—they all dressed well and looked happy in the pictures their relatives showed with pride. These foreigners were often older and not particularly good-looking, but Lorenzo himself was no spring chicken. What was I doing with an old *Cuban* guy who didn't have five ounces of coffee in his apartment? An apartment that wasn't even a real apartment, but a couple of rooms in a decrepit house?

In the twenty minutes or so it had taken us to get to the hotel, my love for Lorenzo had dwindled, crushed under the exotic appeal of Santiago de Compostela. Kiel didn't actually look half bad once you noticed his pretty eyes and perfectly aligned teeth. I would get used to his appearance. I might even learn his language and go with him to visit his relatives in Mariager, wherever that place was.

THE "BUNGALOW" HAD BEEN a little granny house a block away from the Comodoro Hotel. Inside, the air was stale. A coffeemaker, two dirty glasses and a pile of books cluttered a nightstand.

"Make yourself at home, Mircedidas."

I hated the way he botched my name. He took off his coat, dropped it on a chair and disappeared into the bathroom, leaving me alone in that messy, ugly room.

Kiel's sheen of wealth had led me to expect something better—a suite with nice paintings on the walls, maybe a bottle of wine. Not *that*.

His coat pockets had looked heavy. I heard water running in the bathroom and tiptoed over to the chair. It must have been nerves because I wasn't the snooping type.

In one pocket, I found a cellphone and a small leather notebook that Kiel carried everywhere—I had seen it at Lorenzo's before—with names and numbers scribbled in a language I didn't know. In the other pocket was his wallet, with credit cards and a thick wad of bills. Mostly American dollars but there were other notes I didn't recognize. I put everything back, fighting the desire to slip a couple of fifties into my purse that he wouldn't miss anyway. (I am happy to report that I didn't sink that low.)

Kiel finally came out, wrapped in a big green towel. His arms and upper chest had been covered in patches of skin grafts. It wouldn't have been too bad if he hadn't been so self-conscious, but he had been clearly uncomfortable, and that had made *me* uncomfortable too. I took off my clothes, and we got in bed and kissed again, but as hard as he tried, he couldn't get it up.

I was a pretty attractive girl, but maybe not his type.

Or it was possible that he felt guilty about Lorenzo. The whole thing had been embarrassing, though probably more for him than me. When it became clear that nothing was going to happen, he called me a Panataxi, and I got out of there as fast as I could.

I didn't want to show up in a taxi, in case Mamina saw it. Panataxis charged dollars or CUCs, which she knew I didn't have. I had asked the driver to stop in front of a bar that was just a few blocks away from the house. Not ready to face my grandma, I went in and ordered a beer, then another, trying to drown the memory of what had happened at that dingy "bungalow" and to silence my conscience. How could I have done that to Lorenzo? How was I going to look at The Viking again? Feeling ashamed and like a total *puta*, I kept drinking until night fell. Mamina was horrified when I finally made it home. She thought I had had a fight with Lorenzo. I didn't set her right.

Afterward, Kiel and I avoided each other. He didn't visit Lorenzo as often as he had before. If he dropped by, I made an excuse and left. A few months later, I started going out with Nolan. My relationship with Lorenzo came to an abrupt end, and I never saw The Viking again.

And yet the idea of finding my mother, stirred by our

brief conversation, was still beating like a small, secret second heart. It might have influenced my decision to leave Lorenzo for Nolan, though I soon found out that not even Sherlock Holmes could have located my mother in a country of three hundred million people. Particularly when we didn't have a first or last name.

No one ever knew of my adventure, or rather mis-adventure, with The Viking. Unsuspecting Lorenzo once complained about how "aloof" I acted when Kiel was around. The fight they'd had—if Javier was telling the truth—couldn't have been about me.

I finally found the elevator and pushed the button to the seventh floor, which, according to a sign on the wall, was the promenade deck.

11: On the Promenade Deck

The promenade as such was an outdoor walkway that wrapped around the ship. People had gathered on the deck to watch the scenery. Within reach but not quite, with its crumbling façades, huge trees, and the long Malecón seawall, was Havana, the city that Lorenzo had loved and known so well. I could still hear him chronicling its history, exuding a secret pride for having been born there.

"San Cristóbal de la Habana was founded in 1515, plundered later by pirates and corsairs, named the Key to the Gulf, occupied by the British and then returned to Spain—Have you ever thought, Merceditas, that if Britain hadn't gotten Florida in exchange for Havana, thanks to the Treaty of Paris, today we'd be speaking English? That instead of black coffee, you would be drinking tea?"

To our right was the Morro Castle; to the left, the white dome of the Capitol building. "Similar to the American Capitol, only bigger, with European-style gardens and a grand Hall of Lost Steps that once housed a twenty-five-carat diamond. A diamond formerly owned by Tsar Nicholas II!"

I shook my head to silence Lorenzo's voice. Sometimes it bothered me when he pontificated that way—as it would happen later with Nolan. But more often I listened, enthralled, because he had a way of making history come alive. But *he* wasn't alive now, I reminded myself. And that could be my fault. Or not.

"*Lo pasado, pisado*," I muttered.

Some guy was avidly snapping pictures—one of those sickos who'd traveled to Cuba to indulge in our misery and then display it for the world to see. The terminal building was a big square box of concrete with dirty walls. Why would anybody want a photo of it? And yet he wasn't the only one. Many others clicked away as if they were facing the Mona Lisa. "Poverty porn," Nolan called it.

Javier materialized by my side. It creeped me out how he managed to know exactly where I was among the thousand or so people on board.

"How are you feeling, Merceditas?" he asked.

"Like shit."

We started walking together. I noticed again the limp in his left leg.

"Your husband wasn't happy, eh?"

"He's very stressed."

"Hope he didn't mind that we were talking."

"No, not at all."

He leaned closer and whispered, "I bought an Internet package and googled Yordanka. Her name isn't on the Casa de las Américas directory. She *does* use a Gmail address, though Casa has its own server."

Though I had already suspected it, the confirmation of my fears hit me like a punch in the gut.

"And most passengers here don't speak Spanish," Javier went on. "Who's going to take a creative writing course with me aboard the *Narwhal*?"

I took a breath and looked around. "Yordanka and Doctor Fernández are someone's creations, Javier. And that person is up to no good."

That person, however, could be Javier himself. I decided to be vigilant and try to catch him in a lie while pretending to go along with his story.

A corner of his mouth twitched. "You still think it's The Viking?"

"I'm not sure anymore. The truth is, Kiel has had plenty of time and resources to harm us all these years. Why now? And even then, to avenge Lorenzo—after he killed him, like you said?"

"*You're* the one who said someone was after us," Javier reminded me. "I hadn't thought of him or Lorenzo in a long time."

Yes, I had been the one making paranoid, perhaps seemingly crazy assumptions. Until all of those dots connected to form a terrifying shape, justifying my concerns.

A bubbly waitress came out with a tray of drinks and started passing them around. Javier flinched and stroked his left side.

"*Ay*, my hip hurts more than ever this morning."

Curiosity finally got the best of me.

"What happened to your leg?"

"I got in a bad car accident two years ago."

That must have been 2015. The same year Selfa's son had died—

"It was a hit-and-run in Madrid. Luckily, I ended up with just a shattered hip after my VW was totaled. But I needed three surgeries, couldn't walk right afterwards and had to quit my travel writing. Between my health problems and the crisis in Spain, I wasn't making it, so I moved to Miami. Unfortunately, the job situation hasn't improved."

The Grateful Dead fan came by.

"We're trapped here!" he said in Spanish, fingering his gold chains. "*¡Que mierda es esto!*"

"Don't worry." I faked a smile. "Nautilus doesn't want to lose business. They know better than to piss off their clientele."

"I should have bought a plane ticket instead!"

He went away spitting *coños* and *carajos*.

No one else was around, but I spoke in a hushed tone. "What if Lorenzo went to sleep after the fight with Kiel or whoever? He might have lit a candle and forgotten it."

"I doubt it, Merceditas. It wasn't dark enough for him to need a candle. He couldn't have fallen asleep so fast, either. I wasn't at Carmela's restaurant for more than forty-five minutes."

Javier stopped and surveyed the small crowd that had gathered around the smiling waitress. I did the same, though more discreetly. I watched *him* too.

"Was there no investigation of his death?" I prodded. "How did the police determine it was an accident?"

"There was an investigation." Javier leaned against the railing. "When I went back to El Paladar a week later, they suspected arson. Carmela told me the police had interrogated Lorenzo's next-door neighbor. Did you know that she had tried to take over his share of the house once?"

"Yes, and I even thought that—"

"She denied everything, saying she wouldn't have risked burning down her own place with her children inside."

I considered it. "Yeah, that makes sense. They shared a wall."

Javier turned around. His face was now at an angle that made it hard to see his expression.

"The police also questioned me. They asked when I had last seen Lorenzo. I said several months before, which was the truth. But I didn't mention I had been in the building on the day of the fire because—well, like I said, I was afraid."

I crossed my arms.

"Kiel was a shy guy," I said. "He and Lorenzo didn't roughhouse or call each other names, even jokingly, like some guys do. I can't see them fighting to the death."

"Don't kid yourself, Merceditas. I don't know about the Dane, but Lorenzo had a bad temper. They could have been arguing, and if things got out of hand—"

I shook my head, unconvinced. Lorenzo's chats with Kiel had always sounded like lectures: scholarly, polite and dull as a twice-told tale. They only talked about books and history and abstract matters that didn't lend themselves to heated discussions. What would they argue about? Cofiño and Sholokhov?

Me, said a tiny, guilty voice, but I ignored it.

"Who could have hated Lorenzo enough to kill him?" I asked, more to myself than Javier. "Because if it wasn't The Viking, and I can't really see . . ."

A ripple of panic flickered over his face. I couldn't tell if he had seen someone or had had a scary thought. He just stood there, frozen.

"Javier?"

"Have you—?"

He fell silent. When he tried to speak again, only a croaking sound came out. I waited, but he kept staring over my shoulder.

"What's going on, *chico*?"

"That—that dude was getting way too close."

The skinny "hippie," wearing a long-brimmed hat, walked away from us with his hands placed on his lower back. He seemed harmless. Just a typical tourist. A big, expensive-looking camera hung around his neck.

"See you later, Merceditas," Javier said out of the blue.

With that, he left, limping away fast. I watched him go, stunned, trying to figure out what in the world had gotten into that *pendejo*.

AFTER A WHILE I went back to the guest service area. It was less crowded than early in the morning. Frightened and confounded by Javier's hasty departure, I suddenly decided to take a chance and just . . . ask. Talk to someone who could do, or at least know, something. I addressed a uniformed guy sitting behind a massive desk with a computer in front of him.

"Has Selfa Segarra showed up?" I tried to sound casual.

His eyebrows rose.

"No, she hasn't, madam. Do you know her?"

"We are old friends—well, more like acquaintances. When we met yesterday in the boarding queue, she was very nervous. I was wondering if she came on board after all."

"We are not sure. She was issued an ID card but didn't report to her muster drill. That's why we have been calling her. Because until we find her, we can't—" He cut himself off, obviously afraid of having said too much.

I shuffled my feet, uncomfortable, not knowing where to start.

"Ms. Segarra might have decided to leave immediately after getting her card," he added. "It's not a common occurrence but we've had a few cases before.

People get cold feet at the last minute or remember something urgent they have to take care of." He paused and looked at me intently. "You said that she was *nervous*?"

"Yes, she even told me she wanted to 'just go home.'"

"She did! Are you sure, madam?"

"Totally."

He typed something on his computer.

"Do you know if Ms. Segarra had any reason to be worried or upset? Not ready for a cruise?"

I thought of sharing her son's story, but it didn't feel right. *En boca cerrada no entran moscas*, I reminded myself.

"Madam?" The guy turned his face toward me again. If someone seemed worried, it was *him*.

"She had gone through some rough times recently," I said at last. "Family issues. I would say she was a bit depressed."

He nodded eagerly and typed some more.

"Thanks for informing us, madam. Thanks so much! That explains it. She probably never came on board."

He looked relieved. I began to breathe more easily too. I remembered waiting for Nolan after I got my ID card. I could have left the terminal building before going through security and no one would have stopped me, or even noticed. It all made sense. Selfa hadn't actually been on the *Narwhal*. Javier's story might or might not be true. Now if I could just find out about The Viking . . .

"Could you tell me if a man named Kiel Ostargó is among the passengers?" I asked.

"How do you spell his first and last names?"

I had never seen them in writing. I did my best, but after several attempts the clerk gave up.

"Sorry, madam. None of them corresponds to anyone on our passenger list."

"That's okay," I said lightly. "I just thought I had heard an acquaintance's name."

I walked away before the guy asked how many "acquaintances" I happened to have on board.

While I waited for the elevator, a new announcement came over the intercom. Disembarkation would start in half an hour on deck three. I hurried to our stateroom and found Nolan waiting for me impatiently, ready to go.

PART III:
Las Perseidas

1: Old Havana

Though I was relieved about Selfa, Javier's latest revelations and the way he had fled still baffled me. But no way was I going to bring it up again with Nolan. Let sleeping dogs lie, right? *No revolver la mierda, que sale mal olor.* I also found it odd that my comments about Selfa's nervousness had been taken at face value. How did that clerk know I was telling the truth? Well, it wasn't my problem. The *Narwhal* officers were likely happy to have a reason to dismiss the incident and go on with the program before pissed-off passengers staged a mutiny.

On deck three, we were again divided into "Cubans and other foreigners" and "Americans only." But the disembarkation process wasn't nearly as smooth as the previous day's queue. People had grown impatient. There was some pushing and shoving, and plenty of cursing too. Order wasn't restored until the burly guys in white uniforms showed up.

I took my place at the end of the short non-American queue. The hippie was first in line, followed by Grateful Dead. Suddenly I spotted Javier in a corner, watching the waiting passengers but not showing any intention to join them.

"*¡Oye, comemierda!*" I yelled, running toward him.

The Argentinian couple turned to me. So did Grateful Dead.

"Why did you take off like that? *Ni que hubieras visto al diablo.*"

Javier put a finger on his lips and whispered, "I think I had a panic attack. All the memories and . . . you know. Sorry."

"Was that it?"

"Ah, yes."

We looked at each other for a few seconds. He still wore the same scared expression as before.

"It seems like Selfa didn't come on board after all," I said.

I would have told him more, but he was clearly uninterested, keeping an eye on the disembarkation line.

"Aren't you getting out, Javier?"

"What for?" he said after some hesitation. "There's no point in taking a taxi to Casa de las Américas if Yordanka isn't there."

"Are you planning to stay here all day?"

He shrugged. "At least food is free. The library and the bars are open. It's not like I need to 'discover' the city or anything. And who knows? Yordanka may get back to me."

The non-American line moved. So did the American. With order reestablished, the guys in white uniforms left.

"Bye, Merceditas."

Javier trailed after the security guys.

When my turn came, the Cuban customs officer took a quick look at my two passports and said, "Welcome back, Mercedes!" Easier than at the José Martí International Airport, where you had to go through two checkpoints.

Three tourist buses waited outside the Sierra Maestra Terminal building. Nolan and I hadn't bought any shore excursions, but one was offered free "to compensate for the inconveniences."

The *Narwhal* program director, a frazzled woman who introduced herself as Liz, encouraged everybody to board the buses.

"This is a fantastic opportunity to discover Old Havana," she gushed. "You'll get a ride to Cathedral Square—a very short drive, but with amazing views—and participate in a guided tour of the cathedral itself, then visit a nearby gallery to chat with local artists. They have now an exhibit inspired by Alejo Carpentier's work. It's called *Lo Real Maravilloso*."

Nolan's eyes lit up. He liked Carpentier's novels almost as much as he did Cofiño's.

"All that as part of our people-to-people package!" Liz concluded, breathlessly. "We hope you guys enjoy it!"

"Let's get on a bus," Nolan said. "It'll be easier to find a taxi at Cathedral Square."

I'd have rather gone directly to Mamina's house, but we didn't have much choice. There were no other vehicles around. The port area was a no-parking zone.

Once on the bus, I recognized the couple that had tried to arrange the *almendrón* ride the day before. No one else I knew, for which I was grateful.

Our route followed the sea for several blocks. The program director pointed out the Morro Castle and the marble statue of El Cristo silhouetted against the sky. It was beautiful, but I kept my eyes off the road. I hadn't visited this part of the city in around nine years. Every time I returned, I went straight from the airport to Miramar and managed to avoid Old Havana altogether.

Five minutes into the drive, Nolan's phone buzzed,

announcing an incoming text. He read it and his face relaxed.

"It's from Doctor Fernández!" he said. "We're going to meet at six-thirty at La Madriguera."

"I thought that the lecture was going to be at the Faculty of Arts and Letters."

"La Madriguera is just a couple of blocks away, at La Quinta de los Molinos."

La Quinta was a big park where trees and bushes grew in clusters, making it look and feel like a pint-sized forest. La Madriguera—a building that housed an art gallery and a small auditorium—was tucked away at the north end. I had visited it once with Lorenzo. We had entered La Quinta and walked through a scruffy area, tiptoeing around water ponds, broken statues and overgrown shrubbery. A hooting owl had scared the daylights out of me. There had been something dis-quieting about the place. It wasn't what you expected right off a busy street like Salvador Allende Avenue.

"La Madriguera is more like a gathering spot for artists," I said. "Why would you want to give a lecture there?"

"Because the university is closed until classes start in September. And remember, today's Sunday."

"May I see the text?"

He rolled his eyes and handed me the phone.

The message, in Spanish, came from a restricted number and read:

SEE YOU TONIGHT AT 6:30 AT LA MADRIGUERA. STUDENTS ARE EXCITED TO MEET YOU. THE PRESS WILL BE THERE TOO, A REPORTER FROM JUVENTUD REBELDE! SORRY THE FACULTY BUILDING IS UNAVAILABLE, BUT LA MADRIGUERA IS A FABU- LOUS VENUE AND LOTS OF PEOPLE WILL ATTEND, NOT JUST COLLEGE KIDS. DIRECTIONS ARE BELOW.

I'D DISCOVERED LA MADRIGUERA when the Hermanos Saíz Association—a young writers and artists guild— invited Lorenzo to read at their literary *tertulia*. He had shared an excerpt from *Las Perseidas*. That was the first time—the only time, actually—I heard him read aloud.

The Perseid meteor shower is the ghost of a comet. Burning particles of a fiery snowball that left us long ago. The Swift-Tuttle pays a visit to our solar system every 133 years. The last time was in 1992; its tracks are still fresh. For in each visitation, it leaves billions of calling cards, freckles of stardust that flash across the sky when the Earth passes through them. Even if it seems like the tiny meteors are coming toward us, hailing from the constellation Perseus, the Hero, that's an illusion. It's us, the entire planet, that runs into its arms.

At the end, the audience had burst into applause. Lorenzo's face was radiant, framed by dark hair that touched his shoulders and gave him a bad-boy maverick appeal. So many girls had swarmed around him like literary moths before the night was over that I, though not the jealous type, had joined him and looped my arm possessively through his.

THE BUS STOPPED A few blocks away from the cathedral. The local guide, a twenty-something, energetic and overly enthusiastic guy named Yotiel, was waiting for us. He spoke good English, or at least it sounded good to me, throwing in phrases like "you know" and "I mean." He seemed at ease with American tourists, and Liz assured us we were in good hands, before making herself scarce.

There were still no taxis around, so Nolan and I followed our party and started strolling toward the cathedral's bell towers.

"They are asymmetrical," Yotiel remarked, "which is a clear baroque sign."

He kept pointing to old buildings whose "colonial charm" and peeling walls made my companions *oh* and *ah*. We encountered sellers peddling Che figurines, *almendrón* models made of soda cans, baseball bats, realistic-looking machetes (with sharp blades and hardwood handles) and necklaces of seeds and shells.

A *florista* approached us, carrying roses, gladiolus and gardenias in a metal bucket. The *Narwhal* crowd came buzzing around her. A woman in a wide-brimmed Panama hat dusted off her Spanish to address her.

"*¿Cuánto las flores, por favor?*"

"The roses, three dollars the dozen; all others, just two dollars," the flower vendor answered in English.

Gardenias' sweet, intoxicating aroma had once been the fragrant symbol of Lorenzo's love. I inhaled longingly but stayed away from them.

Yotiel was still talking.

"Let's turn on Mercaderes Street, named after the many stores that used to exist in the area in the seventeenth and eighteenth centuries. *Mercaderes* means 'merchants' in Spanish."

An old black man dressed as a slave was sitting on a bench, impersonating Taita Julián, the protagonist of a

Cuban soap opera. My companions found him "lovely" and "picturesque." I cursed them silently, getting hot and bothered as we walked under the three o'clock sun.

The next street, aptly named Empedrado, was cobbled, which proved to be a challenge for our already tired and sweaty party. Yotiel noticed and slowed down.

"And here's the cathedral, the Great Dame of Old Havana! The crown jewel of Eusebio Leal, our beloved city historian! If we have a chance later, we'll visit his office."

Eusebio Leal had been a habitual presence at the Faculty of Arts and Letters. He was bright and entertaining, but his voice, low and honeyed, had a Valium-like effect on me. Yotiel took after him.

"Notice, ladies and gentlemen, the swirling façade described by Alejo Carpentier as 'music turned to stone.' The cathedral currently serves as the seat of the Roman Catholic Archdiocese of San Cristóbal de la Habana and houses the San Carlos and San Ambrosio Seminary."

"Are priests still ordained in Cuba?" the woman in the Panama hat asked.

Yotiel nodded emphatically.

"Yes. Not too many, but there's a vocational crisis in the Catholic church throughout the world."

A dance troupe came down the street. The women wore feather headpieces and sequined dresses, and the men, white drill shirts and straw hats. They moved rhythmically to a recorded soundtrack of drums and trumpets.

"These amazing dancers were part of last month's carnival's parade," Yotiel said. "Now they are honing their skills for the next event."

"You had carnivals in July?" a white-haired woman asked, wiping her forehead with a lavender-smelling handkerchief. "It must have been awfully hot."

"My dear lady, we're children of the tropics," Yotiel answered. "We love to play under the sun!"

We? I wanted to tell him to speak for himself. But why rain on his parade?

"Indeed, carnivals used to be held before Lent, in February, like they are in other parts of the world, but the date was changed to pay homage to our country's recent history," he went on. "They now start around July 26, to celebrate another anniversary of the attack of the Moncada Barracks that sparked the revolution."

"Carnivals have been turned into a *communist* holiday?"

Yotiel pretended not to notice the intention. Either

he had been instructed not to argue with tourists over politics or didn't want to risk losing a tip.

"They're just a *fun* holiday. Today's carnivals include a parade of beautiful floats and *muñecones*, life-sized puppets that are enjoyed by children and adults alike. I'm sorry you missed the chance to see them this time. But maybe next year! Ah, here we are."

We were in front of the cathedral. The façade was imposing, with solid, elegant columns, but our group didn't show much interest.

"Let's get in!"

"This is hot, man."

"Whose idea was it to walk all the way here anyway?"

"Please, come inside," Yotiel said. "Be careful and watch for small irregularities on the floor. Feel free to take an issue of *Vida Cristiana*, a weekly newsletter published by the Jesuits. You can read it and practice *su español*. While you rest, I'll tell you about this remarkable building. See how the central arches are buttressed by eight stone flying arches? Over there is a sculpture of San Cristóbal, patron saint of Havana."

Nolan followed our guide and entered the cathedral. He seemed to have forgotten we had only gone to Old Havana to take a taxi to my house. Reluctantly, I came in too and sat next to him on a hard pew.

2: "All Things Are Passing"

The inside of the cathedral felt like a warm cocoon. The combination of the dark space and Yotiel's sugary voice made me sleepy. I started to drift off. Suddenly, perhaps due to the sweetish sandalwood fragrance that filled the temple or the potent smell of roses somebody had brought in, I felt like vomiting.

Ay, no! Not here! How embarrassing! Lorenzo would never forgive me . . . I mean, Nolan wouldn't.

A deep breath didn't help. I *was* still a bit drunk. Both drunk and hungover. A sad-faced saint painted on the wall glared at me.

Nolan was spellbound listening to Yotiel.

"I'm going outside," I muttered.

"What for?"

There was no time for explanations. I got out in a hurry. Nolan followed me and saw why I'd needed to leave. We moved away from the mess I had left under the baroque portico.

"We can walk around until you feel better," he offered.

"No, I don't want to walk. I want to go home."

"Home? Back to Gainesville?"

"To Mamina's house! I'll find a taxi, an *almendrón* or something."

A smartly dressed man came over. He wore blue jeans and a crisply pressed light-blue shirt. He was tall, brown-haired and handsome. I noticed all that without paying much attention, or at least without paying attention in an obvious way, using that radar for good-looking guys that most women have. Mine had been pretty much out of use during the last few years.

"Excuse me," he said in just slightly accented English. "I don't mean to interrupt, but if you need a ride, I have a superb *almendrón* waiting nearby. A 1958 Chevy Impala, very comfortable."

Nolan and I exchanged a glance.

"*¿Cuánto hasta* Miramar?" I asked.

"Fifteen dollars."

"*Bueno*," I told him. And to Nolan, "Let's go, *papito*."

He shook his head.

"I'd rather stay for the rest of the tour and see that *Lo Real Maravilloso* exhibit."

My neck muscles tensed.

"But it'll do you good to rest," he went on. "I'll call you before meeting Doctor Fernández."

"La Madriguera isn't safe!" I snapped. "Did you forget what I said?"

"Honey, you're not feeling well." He lowered his voice, and the *almendrón* driver moved a few feet away to give us privacy. "I *do* remember what you said this morning, but it simply doesn't make sense."

"Javier—"

"Forget Javier! That Spaniard was drunk as a skunk."

And so were you, he was probably thinking. I looked down, embarrassed. No wonder he didn't take me seriously.

"Are you ready, folks?" the driver asked. "I can't stay here too long, or they will think I'm harassing tourists."

"They" were two cops who kept a watchful eye on us.

We all started walking away from the cathedral.

"If I see something suspicious, I'll call a *miliciano* immediately," Nolan said. "They're everywhere."

But Cathedral Square was a busy tourist place. La Quinta de los Molinos wasn't.

"You think I'm crazy." I sighed.

"Like I said, you're *overreacting*, Mercy. Please, consider that a press-covered event in Havana will up my chances of being hired at San Diego State. I need all the help I can get. You understand that, don't you?"

I understood how desperate he was. It was all about looking good at the upcoming MLA convention and securing another job. Not that I blamed him. And yet . . .

"Do you still want to cook for us tonight? If I don't have to take Fernández and company to one of those expensive *paladares*, it will save us a bunch."

"I will. But why don't you come with me now?"

He looked at his watch.

"It's already a quarter to four. After the tour is over, I'll grab something to eat and go straight to La Madriguera."

"You can have lunch at home."

"I'd rather not. I don't want to turn up late for the lecture. If I go to your house, Mamina will start talking and fussing over us and it will take forever—"

As if Mamina had ever fussed over *him*!

"I'll see you and your grandmother tonight," he concluded.

I gave up.

"Do you remember how to get there?"

"Not too clearly."

I scribbled the address on the *Vida Cristiana* page over a prayer that began:

> *"Nada te turbe.*
> *Nada te espante.*
> *Todo se pasa."*

All things are passing, right. And I had no reason to feel disturbed, did I? There would probably be a crowd at La Madriguera, like that other time . . .

Nolan put the page in his pocket. The driver led us to a red Chevy Impala that was parked on the curb and opened the passenger door for me. The inside smelled of incense, like the cathedral. The air conditioner didn't work—I didn't expect it would. But once I was out of the sun, it didn't feel too bad.

I waved goodbye to Nolan.

"*¡Ten cuidado!*" I yelled.

He didn't seem to hear me. My last image of him was of his hunched back and craned neck as he waddled toward the "music turned to stone" façade.

3: *Dos Gardenias*

No matter how many years had passed since I'd walked Old Havana's streets, I remembered enough to recognize a patterned tile here, an old fountain there and some stained-glass panels over aged doorways. Above all, I could still walk around at night with my eyes closed and find a certain building . . .

My entire body felt weak when we drove by the corner of Prado Avenue and Trocadero Street. If we had turned right on Trocadero and kept going for two blocks, we would have seen the place Lorenzo used to live.

I remembered his neighbors and their frequent squabbles: Bárbara, with a streak of white in her otherwise dark hair, a big behind and an attitude to match. Her two boys played loud video games that made Lorenzo knock on her door at night or yell through the walls to make the noise stop. He also bickered with her about cleaning the common hall and the staircase.

And then there was Yulisa, Bárbara's older daughter, who borrowed books from Lorenzo and had a crush on him—puppy love. She was tall for her age (eleven or twelve), with long, uncoordinated arms and legs and curly hair.

I longed to know if the building was still painted the same dark blue. If the staircase still smelled faintly of gas. If the long, narrow hall was covered with graffiti, the handiwork of Bárbara's kids. But no use thinking about that run-down place or those people, who probably didn't even live there anymore. Even if they did, they wouldn't have the slightest interest in talking to me.

Lo pasado, pisado.

But the smell of gardenias, or the ghost of a smell, was still lingering in the air. For my birthday on February eighth, Lorenzo had always presented me with two freshly cut flowers. If we happened to be in the apartment, he would procure them seemingly out of nowhere, like a magician. How did he manage to keep them around or bring them in without me noticing? He was sneaky too.

If it was a weekday, halfway through a lecture at the Faculty, someone would come in and say coyly, "Excuse me. I have something for Merceditas, from a secret admirer." The professors, particularly the women, cooed. Girls squealed, delighted. Boys rolled their eyes. The gardenias' smell would fill the classroom—thick, sweet and at times overwhelming, like our love.

When inspired, Lorenzo serenaded me with Isolina Carrillo's most famous bolero, "*Dos gardenias*." And a good voice he had. A baritone voice.

If we had had a fight, which was rare, he would quietly leave gardenias by my side. That was his way to signal it was over. The flowers were always well received, their perfume enough to dissipate whatever little grudge or resentment I was carrying. Except for the last two, which ended up crushed and discarded on the Zapata Street bus stop the last day I saw him.

Lorenzo got his salary in pesos but scraped to buy a few dollars every month. That was the only way we could occasionally have dinner at a private restaurant. We called such nights our "*paladar* dates." Yes, he knew how to treat a lady, even if the lady was a silly girl who understood little about life or love.

El Paladar de Carmela, where he often took me, was just steps from his home. Though I didn't like the food—Mamina was a much better cook than Carmela, who fried everything to a crisp and used too much salt—there was something special about sitting at a table and being waited on.

I looked out the window and noticed we were passing by El Parque Central. A statue of José Martí in white marble presided over it, surrounded by palm trees. A gaggle of old vociferous guys in La Esquina Caliente, who I knew would be talking baseball. It really was a "hot corner" because tempers flared and fights erupted easily. Was it right for Yasiel Puig to defect? Was Havana's team, Industriales, better than its eternal rival, Santiago de Cuba's Avispas?

People waited for the regular buses that stopped in the park, which had become a more touristy spot than I remembered. There were double-decker open-top sightseeing buses waiting for foreign passengers. Colorful *almendrones* hovered nearby. Street vendors walked around offering *paletas*, peanuts and straw hats.

I dialed Mamina's number and told her I was on my way.

"*Niña*, are you hungry?" she asked, as usual.

Other than a cup of watery coffee early in the morning, I hadn't had anything else. Drinking wine, *medias de seda* and a few salt-and-sugar-rimmed margaritas didn't count.

"I'm starving."

"Do you want me to make *arroz con pollo imperial* with melted cheese on top for you guys?"

I would have preferred something different than *arroz con pollo*, but Mamina had probably already started it.

"Perfect. Just for me, though. Nolan's busy."

"Hurry up, sweetheart! I can't wait to give you a hug!"

She didn't mention Nolan. She still resented him because of how much she'd adored Lorenzo. It broke her heart when I left him. He liked her too and once gave her a gardenia cutting that we planted in our backyard.

The driver turned onto Reina Street. We were entering Centro Habana. I lowered the car window. The fresh air did me good.

Now that I was almost sober, I began to find holes in Javier's account. Like why he hadn't told the police what he'd heard on the night of the fire. He didn't need to accuse anyone, just mention that there had been a fight inside the apartment. He could have even done that from Barcelona, where nobody could throw him in jail!

And Kiel? He had regretted our attempted affair, I was sure, as much as I had. He'd had no reason to harm Lorenzo. But Javier had. He'd been, in fact, the only person who had benefited from Lorenzo's death.

Estate tranquila, said Candela's voice in my head. I even heard the tinkling of her silver charms. *Trust the universe.*

"Do you mind if I play some music?" the driver asked, turning to me.

"Not at all."

He pressed the radio's button on the wooden dashboard. A baritone filled the car, sending chills through my spine: *Dos gardenias para ti . . .*

When I glanced at the driver, I realized that his hair was longish and dark, like Lorenzo's. And he wore it like Lorenzo at times, up in a loose ponytail.

4: Villa Santa Marta

Centro Habana became a blur of other cars, the occasional eighteen-wheeler, motorcycles, bicycles and crowds waiting for buses. Once we were in Miramar, the neighborhood where I'd grown up, the city started to resemble an American suburb with fewer people and more modern vehicles.

The *almendrón* stopped right in front of my house. The once-ivory stucco was cracking and peeling in more areas than not. So many of the wrought-iron letters over the gate had been lost that "Villa Santa Marta" had turned into "Villa Anta Ara." It had never looked like a happy place, but the neglect was now more obvious and painful than ever. One more thing to worry about.

Before I got out of the car, the driver introduced himself as Satiadeva—*What kind of name is that?* I thought—and asked how many days we were planning to stay in Havana.

"Because I can be at your service," he said. "Just let me know half an hour before, and I'll pick you up here or wherever you are."

"We're leaving tomorrow," I answered, though a part of me, the scared, suspicious part, had already decided that I wouldn't go back to the *Narwhal*. Not that night, maybe not even in the morning. We would spend the night in Villa Santa Marta and take a plane back to Miami, no matter how much the tickets cost.

Satiadeva handed me a card.

"Here is my phone number," he said. "Call me if you need anything, Señora."

"Okay. Thanks."

The *almendrón* sped up. I walked toward the house. The missing lock had left a gaping hole in the hand-carved gate. The path to the front porch was covered in weeds. The three steps to the porch were so worn out that I jumped over them, afraid that they would collapse under my weight.

The door opened with a screechy creak, and there was Mamina. Old but ageless. Tiny but strong. She shrieked and hugged me tightly.

"*¡Mi niñita!*"

She still called me her little girl, even if I was now

a foot taller and a good forty pounds heavier than she was. Mamina descended from the Taínos, the first inhabitants of Cuba. She had high cheekbones and thick black hair that had grayed little over the years, though she had left seventy behind.

The living room was dark and not precisely inviting. An upright piano that had never been played by anyone in my family stood somberly against a wall. The faded brown leather sofa was covered in dust. The picture window had a broken glass panel. A general air of abandonment permeated the place.

The formal dining room was in better shape, still nicely furnished with an oval oak table surrounded by eight matching chairs. A buffet, a hutch and a china cabinet completed the set. A chandelier lamp with only two functioning lightbulbs hung from the high ceiling, where cobwebs had created a canopy. I started to worry about our dinner that evening.

The dining and living room furniture and all the bedroom sets were part of the original household and had been there for sixty years, if not longer. Though they had just looked outdated when I was growing up, time and visiting antique stores with Candela had made me appreciate their true value: they were elegant pieces, most of them handmade in the early twenties.

Candela, who had seen pictures, loved Villa Santa Marta's "old glamour."

She might have liked the backstory as well. The previous owners, the Sotolongo family, had left during the Mariel boatlift, in 1980, and my dad had gotten the house a few years later. But there had been a Sotolongo woman way before—a woman considered by her neighbors to be a witch—who had given the house its name and held court with ghosts at midnight. The woman had died in the house and, it was rumored, her ghost still lingered around, though I had never seen it.

Little had changed inside Villa Santa Marta since my father's times. The only new appliances were those I had bought for Mamina: a big plasma-screen TV set that she had installed in the kitchen, a refrigerator to replace the old Frigidaire, the microwave she refused to use, a rice cooker that she eschewed too, an electric toaster, a mixer and a few smaller gadgets she hadn't bothered to take out of their boxes.

The kitchen—ample and painted white, farmhouse-style—was our favorite room and meeting area. Unlike the windowless and somewhat stuffy dining room, it got plenty of air and light from the backyard. Two copper pots gleamed on the countertop next to a black landline phone. On the wall was an old German cuckoo clock that didn't chime anymore but kept pretty good time. It faced the television, and the bird seemed to look at the screen with a perplexed expression.

The breakfast nook was big enough for four people. It could even accommodate six if we brought in extra chairs. That was where we would eat in the evening because the prospect of cleaning the dining room in the next couple of hours overwhelmed me. I simply didn't have the energy and wasn't about to ask Mamina to exert herself to please "Doctor Fernández." *Pal carajo.*

The fragrance of the rice and chicken filled the kitchen. Ah, that was the real thing, not that crappy stuff they served on board!

"Food's almost ready," Mamina said.

"I'll take a quick bath first." I smelled like a goat after the walk in Old Havana and the vomiting episode.

"Today is a non-water day, but I have a bucket already filled for you."

People prepared for non-water days by collecting it in all available containers.

"I'm famished, though. Do you have anything to hold me over?"

She brought a tall glass of *café con leche* and a plate with saltine crackers. There was mango jam, made with the ripe fruit from our own mango trees, and cream cheese from the dollar store. I devoured everything while we chatted.

Mamina wanted to know what I had been up to recently, though we talked on the phone every week. I gave her a shortened, sweetened version of the latest events. Nolan and I were planning to move to a different city because Gainesville was too hot and crowded. Yes, the cruise had been a wonderful surprise for us too. No, no *niños* anytime soon.

"That Nolo is selfish. He doesn't want more kids because he has two of his own, but what about you?"

"Oh, I can wait a bit longer."

"Until when? I would *love* to have great-grandchildren!"

"We'll see," I said tactfully.

"Ya veremos, dijo un ciego y nunca vio."

Fortunately for me, a ball of shaggy white fur ran in from the backyard and attacked my shoes. I picked up the pup and put her on my lap, where she started squirming and making happy noises. Under her matted coat was a quick, warm tongue. There must have been eyes and a nose there too, though I couldn't see them.

"That's Nena," Mamina said. "She showed up a week ago and made herself at home. It was raining. I didn't have the heart to kick her out."

I was thrilled she had a companion, but that was also

an indication that Mamina was very, very lonely. As a farm girl, she used to have horses and milk cows, but had never been fond of small animals. Growing up, I had begged unsuccessfully for a puppy or a kitten.

"What kind is she, Merceditas?"

"How would I know?"

"Aren't you an expert on dogs now?"

I laughed, doubting that my stint at Pretty and Pampered had made me an expert on anything.

"A Lhasapoo?"

"What's that?"

"A cross between a Lhasa Apso and a poodle."

"Never heard of Lhasas, but she looks poodlesque."

I bounced Nena on my knees. A sparrow flew inside the kitchen and landed on the granite countertop. When the bird flew back out to the backyard, the pup took off.

"She's a pistol," Mamina said proudly.

The cuckoo clock informed me that it was four-thirty. Nolan would still be with the cruise group, visiting the art gallery. I hoped he called me, as promised, when he got to La Madriguera. I also wished the day—the lecture, dinner and everything else—would be over once and for all.

5: Mamina

The morning's chaos had made me forget Mamina's gifts on board. After profuse apologies—though she didn't care in the least about "stuff"—I went upstairs and got in the bathroom.

I hadn't finished undressing when Mamina opened the door (the lock didn't work) and came in with an aluminum pot full of hot water.

"You don't need to do that for me," I protested feebly.

"How are you going to take a bath in cold water? You might get *pasmo*."

A chill? In a place where the average temperature in August was 85 degrees Fahrenheit? But that was Mamina for you. She also covered all the mirrors with sheets when it thundered. Old wives' tales, but what should I do? I just loved her.

She poured the steaming water inside the bucket and made sure it was warm before leaving. I took my bucket bath with Palmolive soap—Mamina's favorite, so I kept her well supplied—and a washrag, then donned one of the clean, sun-dried housecoats that she had left for me behind the door.

I hand-washed my underwear and hung it on the clothesline. It never failed to surprise me how easily I could adapt back to my old Cuban routine. At home in Gainesville, just a week before, I had thrown a fit because the mechanic that Nolan called to fix our water heater took two days to show up.

I had never been more spoiled than when I lived in Cuba. All Mamina had done since she'd come from Pinar del Río was pamper me. We had gotten along well since the beginning because I wasn't a rebellious child and she wasn't a disciplinarian. She sent me to school every day, but if some mornings I didn't feel like getting up, she didn't make a big deal of it and simply let me sleep. She didn't have much to say about my grades, either. Not that I'm blaming my less-than-average results on her! She probably hadn't approved of some of my boyfriends, but might have thought that, not being my birth mother, she didn't have the right to tell me what to do. But she did. I had no mother except her.

The older I got, the more I appreciated Mamina—a

woman who had started raising me at an age when most people retired. She had lost a son to a war and a daughter to cancer but never looked sad, though never particularly cheerful either. She simply accepted life as it came, or was from a more stoic generation.

THE SALAD OF AVOCADO, tomatoes, onions and lettuce was ready. Mamina had tossed in a dressing made with vinegar, oil, lemon, salt and a teaspoon of honey—her secret recipe. After I went through it, she brought the tray with *arroz con pollo imperial* to the table. I took the first bite and grinned.

"How do you make it? Mine never tastes this good!"

"I used lard to fry the chicken. I know that Nolo says lard's not good for you, but what does he know? And I browned the rice before mixing it with the chicken in my old copper pot. Those Teflon things you sent, sorry but they don't do the trick! I added tomatoes, onion, garlic and peppers, and seasoned everything with salt, vinegar and a pinch of cumin. After cooking the rice and the chicken together for forty minutes, I transferred them to another tray and made layers of rice and chicken, adding ham and mayonnaise to each 'floor.' Then I covered everything in shredded cheese and put everything in the oven to melt that."

She talked like an old sorceress about her beloved potions. I listened eagerly, wanting to take notes—it had occurred to me that a book of Cuban recipes would sell better than, well, a novel—but was afraid of interrupting her and breaking the spell.

"The secret is to do everything slow and step-by-step," she concluded. "Like my grandmother used to say, 'You can reach Rome if you walk long enough.'"

"Your recipe is a metaphor for life?"

"Meta—what? Don't throw these Sunday words at me, *niña*."

"It's like a comparison." I laughed, not being too sure myself.

"My recipe is just that—a recipe." She shrugged. "Now eat. You need to put some meat on your bones."

I dove into the scrumptious *arroz con pollo*. Mamina ate her own food with gusto. Nena kept pawing us and getting treats. Mamina blew softly on a piece of chicken breast before putting it in the pup's mouth. She used to do that for me when I was little.

I snapped a picture of Nena and texted it to Candela. It took forever to upload. In the end, I wasn't even sure it had gone through.

It was six when we finished the dessert: *natilla*,

custard sprinkled with cinnamon and raisins and topped with light, fluffy meringue puffs.

I helped Mamina clean the table. After I briefed her on our dinner plans and asked what was available, she told me not to worry.

"I made enough *arroz con pollo* to feed an army, *niña*. See how much is still in the pot? We'll just reheat it and toss another salad when Nolo and his friend are about to arrive."

Reheating lunch leftovers for company didn't sound right to me, but I chalked that up to becoming too Americanized. After all, we were in Cuba, where everything was reused, repurposed and reheated when needed. Mamina wasn't going to throw all that rice and chicken away. Might as well put it to good use.

While she was upstairs taking her daily nap, I washed the dishes, cleaned the kitchen and gave a quick dusting to the living room, making it as presentable as possible. Then I headed to my childhood bedroom that Mamina kept neat, always ready to welcome me.

The cherrywood bed was covered in a clean patchwork quilt. On the dresser sat an oil lamp with a porcelain base that had lit many nights during the frequent special period blackouts. A painting hung on the wall opposite to my bed—the realistic portrait of a girl standing near a rosebush in what could have been our own backyard in happier times. Her black eyes were bright and piercing, her hair a dark rich brown. The roses were deep purple. She looked around ten years old and wore a long white dress, almost like a gown.

When I was a child, I used to think of her as a long-lost relative, though she wasn't, of course—the painting, like everything else, had belonged to the Sotolongos. I named her Martita, after the house. Her presence in my otherwise lonely room had been reassuring. It still was, and I smiled at her.

By then, my fears had somewhat subsided. The old saying *barriga llena, corazón contento* proved true. My belly was full and my heart felt lighter, if not exactly content. Nolan was a levelheaded guy. If he didn't see a reason to be alarmed, then there *was* no reason to be alarmed. No telling what Javier had actually heard when he got to the apartment and what he had made out of it. Lorenzo could have been yelling at Bárbara's obnoxious kids.

It occurred to me for the first time that Selfa might not be the one who had turned Lorenzo in to the Seguridad. I'd *believed* it was her because my friend Julia, with whom I'd kept in touch for a couple of years after leaving Cuba—until she left as well, married to a Romanian or a Ukrainian—had said so. When all that was going on, Julia was still a student at the Faculty of Arts and Letters, and the place had become a rumor mill working overtime. But she could have been wrong. Selfa wasn't the only professor jealous of Lorenzo's trips abroad and writing career. That Literature Department was a vipers' nest. And in the end, Selfa's disappearance wasn't such. She had simply gotten off the ship because she was obviously not in the mood for a cruise.

As for quiet, diffident Kiel, he wouldn't have killed a fly. Though a burly guy too, he was no match for Lorenzo—he would have gotten his ass kicked all the way from Trocadero Street to Mariager.

Lastly, what *would* Alicia know about Nautilus promotions? Nolan was right. All my suspicions seemed far-fetched now, the result of too many margaritas compounded with *medias de seda* and Merlot.

I got in bed, cradling my cellphone. The sheets, drying outside, had that sweet, fresh smell of sun and wind that no fabric softener could ever duplicate. My eyes closed. I fell asleep under Martita's intense gaze.

6: Positive Thinking

After what felt like a short nap, I woke up rested but a bit groggy and disoriented. When I passed by Mamina's door on my way to the stairs, I heard her talking—she had another landline phone in her bedroom. She was likely filling her friend Catalina in on the latest developments.

"So Merceditas says they're waiting to have children, but I don't know how long *he* can wait—"

The truth was that *I* didn't want kids. I wasn't ready to be a mother, and Nolan had already had paternal experience, which hadn't turned out too well, if you asked me.

Downstairs, the silence of the house crept around me, making me uneasy. It had always been like that—too quiet, too empty.

I walked out to inspect the backyard. Overgrown weeds aside, it wasn't as bad as I had feared after seeing the building's façade. It looked, in fact, quite good, in a wild, French garden sort of way. The mango and orange trees were bursting with fruit. The citrus scent of their blossoms wafted in the breeze. Mamina's wicker rocker sat on the back porch, an invitation to daydream. The property was surrounded by a wrought-iron fence with an intricate design that made it hard for outsiders to peek in. A healthy bougainvillea had spilled over the fence.

Despite everything, the house, I realized with surprise, had character and charm. I could turn it into a *casa particular*! If Nolan couldn't find another job soon, we would spend at least part of the year in Havana, running the place like an Airbnb and making a little money on the side. Mamina would agree to the idea. I saw myself showing the house to Candela, who would love everything about it.

A ripe mango had fallen to the ground. I picked it up and bit into it. It was so soft and juicy that there was no need to peel the skin. Its sweetness exploded in my mouth, sending me back to my childhood. How many times had I sat here under this very tree to feast on mangoes and fantasize about the future? How many times had I waited for my mother to show up and say she was so sorry she had deserted me?

Nena trotted outside, rolled over in the grass and

demanded a tummy rub. I complied and took a good look at her. Judging by her small white teeth and clear eyes, she wasn't even one year old. She was a cutie, but needed a haircut and a shampoo.

A clothesline was strung between two trees next to the cement sink where Mamina still did her laundry. Marjoram, cilantro and basil grew in kitchen castoffs, from rusty pans to Café La Llave cans. A perpetually waterless fountain had been taken over by grass and wild marigolds, which had actually improved its look. A pair of chirpy sparrows hopped over the remains of a statue—of Athenea, Lorenzo had assured me. Everything had a rustic feel there, in stark contrast to the inside of the house—the marble staircase and the old-world furniture. I imagined the prospective Airbnb guests admiring the "local color" that the backyard provided.

The unmistakable fragrance of gardenias drew me to a glossy green shrub. I caressed the blooms, the leaves, the tall stalks . . . Lorenzo had planted it himself, choosing the spot carefully and giving Mamina detailed instructions on how to tend to it. Gardenias were complicated plants, he had said. This one was thriving.

Well, good for it. I reluctantly walked away and proceeded with the checkup. The south side of the house was fine. The servants' quarters, however, were in bad shape, at least on the outside. I didn't even remember what was inside. Probably just old junk, but it wouldn't hurt to find out.

"Should we go snoop?" I asked Nena.

She wagged her tail encouragingly.

The servants' quarters—Mamina and I still called them that, though we never had any servants—were a plain square building around fifty feet away from the main house. There were no trees in that area; the only nearby plant was a rosebush with purple blossoms that grew right in front of the dust-covered door. I attempted to crack it open, and a big thorn pricked my right index finger.

"*¡Coño!*"

My hand flew to my mouth. I looked up and saw it was getting dark. I'd better start making a salad and setting the table for Nolan and Doctor Fernández. I let out another *coño* and ran back to the house. The cuckoo clock read seven o'clock. My nap had lasted longer than I thought.

I ran upstairs and found my cellphone under a pillow. There were no recent calls, only a text from Candela. *Qué chula.* But nothing from Nolan, who had to be at La Madriguera.

Unless . . .

I blocked the deluge of negative thoughts. Candela was a fan of positivity. "What you think about is what you bring about. It's the Law of Attraction, girl!" That was too far out for me. "So you only need to *think* of a million dollars for it to manifest? *No me jodas.*" To which she would reply that I "didn't get it."

Just in case, I visualized Nolan safely giving his lecture to an attentive crowd of Manuel Cofiño's fans. I called his number with as much "positivity" as I could muster.

"*Papito*, let me know when the event is over," I said when his voicemail picked up.

Mamina came out of her room wearing a red-and-white polka-dot dress and a silver necklace I had bought for her in New Mexico.

"You look classy."

"Thanks, *niña*. I don't want to embarrass you and Nolo in front of your friends."

"You could never embarrass us, even if you wore a muumuu!"

She laughed and followed me downstairs, but I didn't allow her to do any more in the kitchen. I made a salad and began to set the table with the nice silverware we seldom used. She went back to the *niños* issue.

"You better get at it, Merceditas. You're still young, but Nolo's an old goat!"

I listened, nodded, smiled and did my best to keep my thoughts positive while waiting for the phone to ring.

7: La Quinta de los Molinos

T ime dragged by, but Nolan didn't call. At eight-thirty, Mamina turned on the television to watch *Letters from the Heart*, a telenovela she had been following for months.

"It was so nice when people used to write real letters," she said. "Pen-and-paper ones you could touch, not that new electronic stuff that's all in the air."

I had tried to get her a cellphone so we could talk in Messenger or at least text once in a while. She had refused.

"What would we write about, Mamina? We talk every Saturday."

"You're always in a hurry lately."

Ouch. But no way was I about to worry her with our money issues and the astronomical cost of long-distance calls to Cuba.

"I'll only send you 'real' letters from now on," I said.

At nine o'clock, I called Nolan again, but his phone

was still off. I texted him and got no answer. Even supposing that the lecture had started at "Cuban time," around seven, it wouldn't have lasted two hours. How long could you expound on Manuel Cofiño's life and work, *por Dios*?

After a while, Mamina asked if we were supposed to serve dinner for just the two of us or keep waiting for "Nolo" and his friend. Like most old folks, she had a regular eating schedule and didn't like to disrupt it.

"Let's have something quick now," I said, though I wasn't hungry.

She made chicken sandwiches and served them with the salad and a jar of cold mango juice. We talked about repairing the house, which didn't enthuse her, but I didn't bring up my idea of turning it into a *casa particular*. Not yet—I needed to discuss it with Nolan first.

Mamina and I ate together in the breakfast nook. It was pitch-dark outside. We had no patio lights, and neither did our next-door neighbors. I felt guilty for having left her alone in this house, which even under the best of circumstances had always felt a little haunted.

After dinner, I cleaned everything again and surveyed the kitchen table. It looked elegant, with the fine china monogrammed with an "M" and a white tablecloth. We had no idea what the "M" was supposed to mean. Marta, like the house? In any case, it was convenient because I could always say it was Mercedes.

"Should I chill a bottle of wine?" Mamina asked. "They sold one per household on July twenty-sixth. I was going to resell it but we can open it tonight."

She never drank alcohol, and I wouldn't have dared touch it in front of her. Plus, I had had enough of that for the day. And though it was probably a cheap wine, I'd rather keep temptation at arm's length.

"No, thanks. Nolan doesn't drink."

We moved to the living room to wait for the guests. The pendant light didn't work—something had gone wrong with the wiring, Mamina said. She turned on a brass table lamp supported by two chubby cherubs. We sat in the rocking chairs that were, like everything else, "vintage," with carved spindles and busted cane seats. The leather sofa was better avoided; it had angry springs poking through, ready to stab the behind of whoever sat on it. The piano was in the shadows, thankfully, because my quick and dirty dusting hadn't done much for it.

Mamina tried to keep the conversation going, but

her voice was quivery. As the small talk dwindled, she yawned a couple of times. She was used to being in bed by nine-thirty. I hated to keep her waiting.

By a quarter to ten, and after another unanswered call, I'd had enough.

"I'm going to La Quinta de los Molinos," I announced.

Mamina clucked and shook her head. "What are you going to do there, *mija*, at this time of the night?"

"That's where Nolan is giving his lecture."

"But that place is closed now, Merceditas!"

"Not La Madriguera."

"What if Nolo's on his way? He'll be in Miramar by the time you get to La Quinta."

"Then he can give me a call and I'll turn around."

"That's crazy, *niña. ¡Estate tranquila!* Nobody's going to steal that guy from you."

Steal him! If she only knew—I called the *almendrón* driver, who agreed to pick me up in twenty minutes.

"I'm dropping off someone at the Meliá Cohiba hotel, then I'll go straight to your house."

Nolan could have been with Doctor Fernández drinking beer at a *paladar*. Or still at La Madriguera, praising Manuel Cofiño's contributions to socialist realism. He could have forgotten to turn on his cellphone after turning it off before the lecture. But my fears, unfounded or otherwise, were now here in full force.

Satiadeva honked outside.

Mamina came out after me and assessed both the *almendrón* and its driver. Satiadeva had changed clothes and wore dark trousers and a white guayabera. His hair fell down around his face in soft waves.

"So we're going to La Quinta de los Molinos?" he asked, sounding a bit baffled.

"My granddaughter has forgotten how things work here," Mamina said. "Most parks close after eight o'clock. Because La Quinta is like a park, right?"

Satiadeva nodded.

"Yes, Señora. A botanical garden, actually." He turned to me. "Why do you want to go there, if you don't mind my asking? A Santería offering or . . . ?"

"Uf, no! I don't believe in that stuff."

He opened the door and I got into the passenger seat. Unexpectedly, Mamina slid in the car too, settling on the other side.

"I'm not letting you go there by yourself," she declared.

"Come on, I'm thirty years old! What if Nolan comes in while we're both out?"

"Then he can give you a call and *we* will turn around."

There was no way to convince her to stay home. I got out again, wrote a note for Nolan asking him to wait for us, left it at the door while Satiadeva waited patiently, and off we went. In truth, I was grateful to have Mamina around. It had been a long day that might get worse before it was over.

"What's inside that La Quinta place?" Mamina asked before I could tell Satiadeva about La Madriguera. "I've never been there."

"It's a historical site, Señora. The former residence of Máximo Gómez, a general of our Independence War."

"I know who Máximo Gómez was!" Mamina said, offended.

"Oh, I'm sorry. Some people don't. A long time ago, La Quinta used to be a tobacco mill, hence the name. In Spanish colonial times, it was used as a summerhouse by Captain General Miguel Tacón, so it was fitting that Máximo Gómez got it after the Cubans won the war. If we were to visit during the day, you'd see a museum as well as beautiful fountains, charming pergolas and many kinds of birds and exotic trees."

Satiadeva was in full Eusebio Leal mode. It looked like all *almendrón* drivers and tourist guides had studied under his tutelage: low voice, careful pronunciation and a penchant for hyperbole. There weren't any "charming pergolas" or "beautiful fountains" when I had visited, just a thicket of trees, shrubs and stinky ponds.

Once in Centro Habana, Satiadeva turned on Salvador Allende Avenue and stopped in front of the high wrought-iron railings that surrounded La Quinta de los Molinos. I got out of the car. The gate, also made of iron railings, was closed. There was nobody around. A scent of summer floated out of the park—earth, blooming flowers and a faint trace of beer.

"Didn't I tell you?" Mamina followed me.

Satiadeva joined us.

"All right, ladies, what's going on? I'm glad to be of help, but you need to tell me what this mystery is all about."

"There's no mystery," I replied. "My husband is a college professor and was invited to give a lecture at La Madriguera. We're looking for him."

"La Madriguera! Then we're in the wrong place."

"Isn't it inside La Quinta? I remember coming in through it once."

"That must have been a long time ago. Now the only entrance is on Jesús Peregrino Street."

We went back to the car and Satiadeva made a left turn on Infanta Avenue.

Positive thoughts, positive thoughts.

We would find Nolan. The driver knew the city better than I did after so many years abroad. I was never familiar with Centro Habana, being a Miramar girl.

La Madriguera was tucked in at the end of Jesús Peregrino Street. Satiadeva parked on the curb. I hopped out and entered the building through the art gallery. The auditorium where Lorenzo had read from *Las Perseidas* was full of young people, all excited and talking loudly. Music came from an inner courtyard with mural-decorated walls. A tired-looking custodian sat on a bench while keeping an eye on the crowd.

"Is Doctor Fernández around?" I asked him.

"Doctor who?"

"Fernández, from the Faculty of Arts and Letters. He invited my husband to deliver a lecture here. It should be over by now."

The custodian gave me a quizzical look.

"A lecture? We're having a hip-hop concert."

"When did it start?"

"At nine."

"Did you have another event before that?"

"No, we didn't open until eight."

Anxiety rippled through my body. I had been right from the beginning—there was no Doctor Fernández, no lecture, no—

I turned around, walked out and saw Satiadeva, who was waiting for me.

"Can we get inside La Quinta de los Molinos?" I asked him.

"I don't think so, unless we jump over." He pointed to a concrete wall that separated La Madriguera from the park. "And even if we could, you wouldn't even be able to see your own hands there. It could be dangerous."

"Don't they have security guards?"

He chuckled. "What for? Thieves aren't interested in Máximo Gómez's machete or Tacón's hat. By dangerous I mean the ponds. Some are as big as sinkholes. And branches that can hit you in the face if you don't notice them on time—that sort of thing."

With no other option, we walked back to the *almendrón*.

8: Las Perseidas

Before we got to the car, Satiadeva stopped and asked me, "Would you like to try the Faculty of Arts and Letters? That's a more appropriate place for a lecture than La Madriguera."

The Faculty. I felt a blade of pain. Pain and fear.

"How do you know?"

"I used to teach there."

My nerves were a tangle. We got in the *almendrón*.

"What . . . what did you teach?" I stuttered, studying his square jaw and broad shoulders, his longish brown hair.

"English. But I couldn't make ends meet with a salary in pesos. I used all my savings to buy the Impala and became a driver. More profitable."

An aching hollow opened inside me, but I asked in a casual tone, "Did you ever meet Lorenzo Alvear?"

"Alvear," he repeated. "I can't place it, but sounds familiar."

"He taught literature at the Faculty."

Satiadeva started the engine. A strong smell of gasoline filled the car.

"Wasn't he the guy who committed suicide? I heard his girlfriend—a student—left him for a foreigner." I gulped, but he didn't seem to expect an answer. "That was before my time, though. I worked there from 2012 to 2014."

He didn't kill himself because of me, I wanted to cry. *Just ask Javier!* At this particular moment at least, I was ready to accept the Spaniard's version. But then I looked back and noticed Mamina's serious expression. She had a finger over her lips. We all kept silent on the short drive to the Faculty of Arts and Letters.

I had never wanted to return to the place where Lorenzo and I had first met, where we had kissed in empty classrooms and exchanged notes of love. But there we were, at the intersection of Zapata and G Streets. The building was close to El Príncipe Castle, a military fort that had served as a prison. A famous conspirator had spectacularly made his escape from it. "El Príncipe Castle," Lorenzo liked to say, "is our Château d'If."

Satiadeva parked across from the Zapata Street bus stop, a small structure painted blue with a concrete bench and a trash can inside. And the place where Lorenzo and I had seen each other for the last, painful time.

FOLLOWING THE DINNER AT La Roca with Nolan, and after he left Cuba, I avoided Lorenzo. Nolan had expected me to formally break up with him, but I was too much of a chicken to do so. Afraid of a violent reaction that I somehow justified, I waited, not answering his calls or returning to school, hoping he would take the hint. Now that I think of it, my attitude wasn't too different from Nolan's toward his own wife. Only that Lorenzo and I hadn't been married, of course.

Mamina had been instructed to tell him I wasn't home whenever he called, true or not. And before Nolan returned to Miami, it *was* true most of the time. I spent a week with him on Varadero Beach and another week in Cayo Largo. But Mamina, who had pretty much given me free rein in the boyfriend department as long as I slept at home every night, had been furious.

"I'm tired of lying for you! If you're woman enough to go out with that *Americano*, you should be woman enough to tell Lorenzo you are leaving him to his face."

That ranked among the harshest things she'd ever

said to me. Of all my boyfriends—of whom there hadn't been so many!—Lorenzo was her favorite, hands down. She had been looking forward to our wedding and expected the three of us to live together. We had discussed exchanging the too-big, crumbling and cumbersome Villa Santa Marta for a smaller, more modern place, like an apartment overlooking the ocean in El Vedado. She also knew that my involvement with Nolan only meant that I would eventually leave Cuba. And her.

I would have left Lorenzo in limbo, but a legal requirement had forced me to pay one last visit to the Faculty. Since my trip was supposedly for educational purposes, I had to bring to my visa interview proof that I was doing well in college. Nolan had already arranged this with the dean of arts, who handled his FIU summer courses. She wrote a letter stating I was "a promising student." The dean, like most people who knew about the trip, suspected I wouldn't be coming back to the Faculty, or even Cuba. Lorenzo, I thought, would have already caught wind of the story and figured out what was going on.

I had tried to get Julia to pick up the letter for me, but that wasn't allowed. As part of Cuban red tape, I had to sign a document promising to return to Havana once I finished the FIU workshop. On a Friday at close to five o'clock, I sneaked into the dean's office, signed the paper without bothering to read it, grabbed the letter with the University of Havana's embossed seal on the envelope and *ran*. I got my *culo* down the Faculty marble staircase at record speed. Fortunately, classes had already been over and there were no students around, just a handful of professors and administrators.

I crossed Zapata Street to wait for the Miramar-bound bus but hadn't been there ten minutes when a driver slammed on the brakes and a woman yelled, "That crazy guy! He could have been run over!" I looked up, and who was it but Lorenzo, running straight to me with two gardenias wrapped in brown paper?

Absurdly, I had tried to hide behind a lamppost. Lorenzo was panting when he reached me.

"Merceditas! Where have you been? Why aren't you answering my calls?"

There were blue shadows under his eyes. His white guayabera, ordinarily spotless and ironed, was wrinkled and coffee-stained. His long hair was disheveled, his face as withered as the gardenias that had probably been a few days in his office. I looked away when he offered them to me with a shaky hand.

"Sorry, Lorenzo," I muttered. "This—this is over."

"But why? Are you mad at me?" His eyes were filled with tears. That was the only time I ever saw him cry.

"People won't talk to me," he added, his voice cracking. "Everybody at the Faculty—I know they're saying things, but no one wants to tell me. What did I do?"

My future had hung in precarious balance for an eternal second. I saw in a flash of clarity that was the defining moment: stay in Cuba with Lorenzo or discard him to step into a new life abroad. I could have come up with an imaginary grudge or any excuse, and he would have believed it because he wanted to. But it wasn't worth it. Suddenly, this grief-stricken older man looked like a stranger.

"It's over," I repeated.

He noticed the envelope addressed to the United States Interest Section. I hid it in my pants pocket, afraid he would grab it and rip it to shreds. A glint of fury and recognition passed through his face.

"Is it Nolan?" he asked hoarsely.

If you're woman enough to go out with that Americano, *you should be woman enough to tell Lorenzo you are leaving him to his face.*

"Yes," I found the courage to answer. "I'm in love with him now. Please, don't call or talk to me again."

"You're heartless, Merceditas. How can you tell me not to—?"

A bus stopped in front of me then. I quickly boarded it. As other people rushed in, I remember praying Lorenzo wasn't among them.

When the bus finally pulled away, I dared to look out the window. Lorenzo was leaning against the lamppost with the two gardenias crushed at his feet.

THE FACULTY BUILDING WAS dark and the gate closed. When Satiadeva and I approached, a security guard stopped us.

"We're on vacation, folks," he said, looking at us suspiciously. "And a lecture at this hour? Come on!"

It was eleven o'clock. When I glanced again at my cellphone, all hope gone, the battery was almost dead. That could have happened to Nolan! If he had tried to reach me using a Cuban pay phone, the call wouldn't have gone through because public phones didn't have long-distance access.

"Could Nolo be on the ship?" Mamina asked when we returned to the *almendrón*.

I hadn't considered the possibility, but it was quite

unlikely. "We had agreed that he would bring Doctor Fernández for dinner after the lecture."

"But if the lecture was canceled . . ." she insisted.

Nolan and I hadn't discussed *not* going back to the *Narwhal.* The idea had occurred to me after we had parted ways at the plaza. Though it was a long shot and I would rather have gone home, I directed Satiadeva to the Sierra Maestra Terminal building.

Salvador Allende Avenue was deserted. Havana felt like a ghost town until we got to the Malecón area, which, like New York, never sleeps. People were still sitting on the seawall, enjoying the night breeze or gathered around bottles of rum. The waning moon peeked from behind the Morro Castle lighthouse.

We arrived to the dock at eleven-fifteen. Two big ships were berthed there, but the *Narwhal* was nowhere in sight. We couldn't stop anyway. The entrance was closed, with a chain blocking access. A uniformed guard kept watch.

Satiadeva drove away slowly until he found a parking spot two blocks away.

"Are we in the right place?" he asked.

"Yes, but where the heck is our ship?"

I got out of the car. My legs felt weak, and I had to lean on Mamina.

"Falling stars!" she yelled suddenly. "Make a wish, *niña*! Quick, make a wish!"

"Amazing," Satiadeva muttered. "Looks like it's raining fire."

Bright flashes burst through the night sky. Not scattered fireballs like those Lorenzo and I had seen at Bacuranao Beach, but a blast of yellow, blue and violet arrows that melted in the horizon. Fear and longing swirled in my chest. My head throbbed as if all those needles of light were piercing it.

The Perseid meteor shower is the ghost of a comet. Burning particles of a fiery snowball that left us long ago.

The ghost of a comet. The ghost of a man. Cosmic ashes. All those missing people buried in . . . stardust?

"Lorenzo! Lorenzo!"

9: The Morning After

I woke up with a fuzzy memory of what had happened the previous night. Not exactly a blackout, but a void after a certain point in time. I remembered going to La Quinta de los Molinos, La Madriguera, the Faculty of Arts and Letters and, finally, the port terminal building. I remembered the bright streaks of light against the black backdrop of the sky and Mamina's excitement. Then what?

The sun came in through the window. It was past ten o'clock.

I jumped out of bed, washed my face with water from the bathroom bucket and ran downstairs to find Mamina in the kitchen. She was talking on the phone and keeping an eye on the coffeemaker.

"I hope so, but she's stubborn as a mule! Ah, here she is! Call me later and keep me in the loop about the potato thing."

She hung up.

"That was Catalina," she said. "Potatoes are *liberadas* today."

"*¿Liberadas?*" I had forgotten a few Cubanisms.

"They're going on sale without the ration card. She's been waiting since eight o'clock for the store to open and is saving a place for me." Mamina touched my forehead. "How are you feeling, *niña*? You scared me last night!"

"I did?"

"You had a *zambeque*. You didn't seem to know where you were or who I was. Thank God that gentleman, the driver, helped me put you in the back seat, drove us home and carried you to bed."

"What do you mean, carried me to bed?"

The coffee started boiling. A thick morning smell spread through the kitchen and made me feel instantly awake.

Mamina served me a cup of coffee, then added milk and more sugar than I had ordinarily used.

"I couldn't have lifted you," she said. "He brought you to your room."

The image of Satiadeva with my body in his arms made me blush.

"You were crying all the way home. Calling Lorenzo, babbling about him—"

A sip of hot coffee went through my windpipe, and I began to cough.

"What's going on, *niña*?" Mamina's brows drew down. "Earlier, you were asking the driver if he had known Lorenzo. Why?" She sighed and added with a hint of reproach, "Why *now*?"

Another sip of coffee gave me several seconds to choose my words.

"I had a nervous breakdown, Mamina. Coming back has been very emotional."

"You've been back many times before. Why is this different?"

"I can't find Nolan, for one thing. And then—" I bit my tongue, not wanting to frighten Mamina.

En boca cerrada . . .

"And I thought of Lorenzo yesterday when I saw that his gardenia plant was still in the backyard, looking so pretty," I concluded.

"Well, I take good care of it."

"That's great."

"But I don't understand . . ."

"Please, don't make a big deal out of it. I was just worried, and my mind played a bad trick on me."

Mamina was no dummy. She wasn't buying it.

"Now, since Nolan hasn't shown up and we know

nothing about where he is, I really need to go back to the ship," I said, keeping my voice as even as I could.

"The ship, yes! Why wasn't it there last night?"

"It sailed away so passengers could watch the meteor shower from the sea. I had forgotten all about that."

"The meteor shower, eh?"

Mamina shot me a wary glance. It must have been a sixth sense because it was unlikely that she knew about Lorenzo's book. I had never mentioned it to her. But he *could* have. They used to talk a lot.

"It was quite a sight," I said lightly. "By the way, did you pay the driver?"

"No, *mijita*. He said to call him when you feel better."

I hoped that my purse hadn't been lost in the *zambeque*. Mamina told me it was in the living room, where "that gentleman" had left it. My passport and all the cash I'd had in it were there. When I retrieved my cellphone, the battery was dead, and the charger, of course, still on the *Narwhal*. What about Nolan? Was he on the ship too? Or out of commission, like both our phones?

"Why are you so concerned?" Mamina shrugged.

"I'm sure Nolo is having breakfast on board now, wondering where *you* are."

"May God hear you," I said, though I wasn't the religious type.

When you're afraid, I realized, it's easier to look up in case there's someone or something there, willing to lend you a hand.

Satiadeva had left another card on the table with his name, number and an email address. Mamina called him from the landline phone while I finished my breakfast. Then I helped her carry a load of laundry to the backyard sink. It wasn't a lot, mostly housecoats and underwear, but the thought of her washing our heavy bedspreads by hand made me feel guilty. I tried to take the soap away from her.

"This is nothing, *niña*," she protested. "I'll finish in five minutes. It'll take you forever since you aren't used to it anymore."

"I can send you a washer and dryer," I offered.

We didn't have the money to spare, but I would find it, I thought, ashamed at the sight of her thin fingers squeezing the clothes.

"I don't need any of those new machines that you have to program and whatnot."

Nena, who had followed us to the backyard, made

a mad dash toward the fence, barking wildly. I moved the bougainvillea and looked out at the street but didn't see anybody.

"Probably the neighbor's cat," Mamina said. "He loves to tease Nena. Come here, girl!"

But the pup stood by the fence, growling and with her hackles up.

10: "What You Seek Is Seeking You"

Ten minutes later, Satiadeva knocked on the door. He was wearing a gray shirt, ironed blue jeans and his ponytail hidden by an Orioles cap. We shook hands. I feared that after hearing me gabble about Lorenzo, he had made the connection. But it felt shallow and wrong to be worried about a stranger's opinion when Nolan was still missing.

"Nice to see you again, *mijo*!" Mamina came out of the backyard, wiping her hands in a kitchen towel. "Would you like a cup of coffee?"

"Oh, that's not necessary, Señora." He stood at the threshold. "I had breakfast already."

"Come on in!"

He glanced at me, and I smiled weakly. I wished Mamina hadn't invited him, but didn't want to be rude. Driving tourists around must have been hard for a former college professor. Lorenzo had sometimes talked of offering walking tours of Havana to foreigners but had never gotten around to it. He probably thought it would be beneath his dignity in practice.

I offered Satiadeva two fifty-dollar bills and thanked him for helping "us" the previous night.

"My pleasure. I hope you find your husband soon."

"Thanks."

Getting a better look at him in daylight, he strongly resembled Lorenzo. Or did he? His face was more angular, his eyes a lighter shade of brown. Besides, he was around ten years younger than Lorenzo would've been, had he been alive. But surgeries and facial reconstructions could change people's overall appearance, or they did in the movies, anyway. My only experience in that area was getting some Botox on my forehead.

We all walked into the kitchen. As we gathered around the table, strong déjà vu overwhelmed me. How many evenings had Lorenzo and I sat there with Mamina, talking, laughing and making plans? It was during one of these intimate meetings when he came up with the idea of using his apartment as a *casa particular*. Mamina had approved. "You're welcome to live with us any time," she had said.

"You're welcome to come by any time," she told Satiadeva now, pulling me back to the present. "I really appreciate what you did for my Merceditas last night."

"It was nothing, Señora."

"Sorry for the inconvenience," I muttered. "I'm not usually like that. But my husband is missing and—"

I felt tears stinging my eyes and ducked my head, slouching over the table.

"Don't get so upset," Satiadeva said. "He's probably looking for you now."

"That's exactly what I told her!" Mamina brought him a glass of *café con leche*. When she liked people, she insisted on feeding them, no matter what. "Would you like sugar, Sato?"

Sato, for the record, means "mutt." Satiadeva took it in stride.

"This is perfect, thanks." He tilted his head to look at me. "You know the saying, 'What you seek is seeking you'?"

I steadied myself with some effort. "Huh?"

"It's a Rumi quote."

"Rumi who?"

"A Persian poet."

"Ah, I don't even know Cuban poets."

The phone rang, and Mamina hurried to answer. It was Catalina again to report on "the potato thing."

Satiadeva smiled. On second thought, he didn't look much like Lorenzo. He was just a tall guy with longish dark-brown hair. There were thousands of men like him in Cuba. Still, my breathing was going ragged, as if an invisible hand had curled around my throat.

"Who are you?" I asked, my voice tentative.

Another cryptic smile and a one-shouldered shrug. "Like I mentioned, a former English professor. I'm also involved with a meditation group. We've been reading Rumi recently, hence the quote. We meet every week to discuss esoteric books and exchange ideas about topics people don't often talk about. At least here."

Candela would like that, I thought, beginning to ease up.

"How did you get your name, Satiadeva?"

"Well, it's not my *real* name. I went through an initiation a year ago and chose it because it means 'lord of truth.'"

"I see."

"It sounded silly at first, but I've gotten used to it. It's a symbol of the new me."

It was my turn to smile. He was just a quirky New Age type. I had met a few before, friends of Candela's. Hare Krishnas, devotees of Hindu gods and goddesses, zodiac believers, *metafísicos* and *patafísicos*. So the trend had finally reached Havana.

"On another note, if your grandma ever needs

anything, tell her she can call me," Satiadeva said. "I'll be happy to help."

"Thank you so much."

Mamina came back, announcing, "The grocery store is open! I'd like to accompany you and say hello to Nolo, but I don't want to miss the sale. If I get enough potatoes, they'll last me until the end of the month."

"We aren't leaving until six," I told her. "I'll be back after making sure Nolan is okay."

But I hugged her tight when the time came to leave. Her skin was cold and loose, and her arms as thin as a child's. The reality of her aging struck me with a forceful punch. She must have sensed my distress because it took her a while to let me go.

"I'll send you chew toys and dog shampoo for Nena," I told her to lighten the moment. "My pal Candela has tons of bottles."

"Nena doesn't need any special shampoo! Write to me instead. A regular letter that I can read at night and imagine you're here."

"I will."

I kissed Mamina. I also kissed the pup before getting in the *almendrón*.

Satiadeva and I didn't talk much on the way to the dock. "What you seek is seeking you." I repeated every possible mantra to myself. "Trust the universe. *Estate tranquila*. Visualize the best outcome! Manifest your desires. Be positive!"

The *Narwhal* was back, shiny and pretty. I saw her from two blocks away. Her red, yellow and green hull stood out. Docked between the two cargo ships I had seen the night before, she looked like a summer bridesmaid escorted by steelworkers.

Satiadeva parked on the curb.

"They won't let me enter the parking lot," he said. "Do you want me to wait here, just in case?"

"No, thanks."

If Nolan was on the ship, I was about to be on his case. Seriously. Why hadn't he gone to Mamina's house when he knew how worried I was? But if he wasn't on board—and by now, I knew deep in my heart he wouldn't be—I'd have to call the police and onboard security and . . .

I stretched out my hand.

"Goodbye," I said. "It's been nice to meet you."

"Take care, Mercedes."

How did he know my name? Had Mamina told him?

These two must have had quite a conversation while I was having a zambeque.

11: Trocadero Street

The gangplank was down. Several people were getting off the ship. Among them was Alicia, who looked much younger and carefree in civilian clothes. I kept walking toward the *Narwhal* until the sight of a police cruiser and another official vehicle parked in front of the terminal building stopped me in my tracks.

"Ms. Spivey!" Alicia waved from the dock.

I waited until she joined me.

"We've been looking for you and your husband since last night!" she yelled. "Where were you?"

"We—I was at my grandmother's house."

"Ah, that's right, you're Cuban." She relaxed a little bit. "Sorry, it's been so crazy—"

"Is that about us?" I asked, pointing to the cruiser.

"No, no! The captain called the Cuban police because of what happened to the Spanish guy."

Her face darkened.

"What—what was it?"

"Mr. Jurado was found dead last night, in the library, when we returned from the meteor shower watch. A bronze bust fell from a bookshelf and hit him on the head."

The hair on the back of my neck stood up. My breath caught in my throat. I started to shake. Javier was dead. And Nolan?

"So it was . . . an accident?"

Alicia let out a long sigh.

"That's what the captain and the program directors said." She switched to Spanish. "I don't believe it. There were some waves, but not big enough to move a piece that heavy. *Los oficiales* didn't want to hear that, though. Bad for business."

I remembered how quickly they had accepted the possibility that Selfa hadn't come on board. Just because I said she had been nervous! They had been trying to cover their maritime asses then, and were likely doing the same now.

"Then another passenger didn't show up for the head count. What a night!"

"Was it Kiel Ostargó?" I asked.

"No, the guy had a Spanish last name. I think he was Cuban too. Thank God he came back this morning because the staff captain and the safety officers were panicking."

Well, they weren't the only ones.

Alicia shook her head. "It's one thing after another. This cruise was *embrujado*, I swear."

Worse than cursed.

"*Bueno*, I'm happy you're fine." She gave me a faint smile. "They gave us only one free hour, so I'm going to get a few souvenirs. Remember, everyone needs to be back on board by three o'clock. See you and Mr. Spivey soon."

No need to tell her that I didn't know where Nolan was.

"See you."

I watched her go, still too shocked to move. But I had to do something! Even if all this was simply a series of eerie and unexplainable coincidences, I'd get in touch with the Cuban police and ask them to find Nolan before it was too late.

It is too late.

On a whim, I decided to pass by Lorenzo's apartment. Bárbara might still live there. She had to know who had visited him before his death and what had *really* transpired the night of the blackout. That could hold a clue to what had happened on board, and maybe to Nolan as well. Would she tell me? It wouldn't hurt to try. There was also something stirring inside me, a hope—or a dread—I didn't even dare to name. I set off walking, rushing to Trocadero Street as if my life depended on it.

On my way I saw a dark-haired man reading a book at a bus stop. The man, of course, reminded me of Lorenzo. Who or what didn't, at that point?

EL PALADAR DE CARMELA was open. Two couples occupied a table and a guy ate alone. The smells of fried fish and black beans wafted out to the street.

A few feet away from the restaurant stood the old building with its façade now painted a light-rose color. The grocery store still occupied the ground floor. People lingered about, waiting for their ration-card food.

Past the grocery store was a small corridor, then the stairs. Up there, Lorenzo's old balcony. Dresses, pants and slips hung on the clothesline. He had hated such intimate displays. "Tourists might think it's picturesque, but *I* think it's lacking in manners, showing the world your underwear."

Across from the building was a small park with a run-down bench under a *flamboyán* that exploded in bright-red flowers every spring. The park was a sweet place, where neighborhood kids played hide-and-seek during the day and lovers made out at night. Lorenzo and I would sit there in the evenings to people-watch and talk. We called the bench "our little loveseat."

The "loveseat" felt harder than I remembered, but I sat for around ten minutes, mustering the courage to go upstairs. I watched the street, the passersby and the old folks waiting in line or going about their businesses. An image began to haunt me—Javier in the *Narwhal* library, his head broken open like a coconut by the bust of a poet or a writer.

"Was it a metaphor?" I said aloud. "Or a symbol?"

A woman carrying a bag of plantains gave me a funny look.

Time crept on. I fell into a trance, staring blankly at the balcony where those yellowish bras and panties billowed in the wind.

Would you like to stop by my apartment? It's very small, but I have almost as many books as the library.

I finally stood up, passed by the grocery store and began climbing up the stairs. I had almost forgotten

Bárbara. It had occurred to me—against all common sense—that if I pretended years hadn't passed, if I believed Lorenzo was waiting for me, it would magically happen. The past, like the light of stars long gone, would become the present, and I would step into my old life, still a lovestruck girl.

12: Bárbara and Yulisa

The doors to Lorenzo's apartment had disappeared and the space filled with bricks painted the same pink shade of the wall. The place, which used to be brimming with noises from the TV at full blast and kids arguing or laughing, was strangely quiet. I walked to the end of the hall, where Bárbara lived, and rang the bell.

She opened the door. Her white streaks had spread, covering practically her entire head, and she was ten pounds heavier. Other than that, she looked the same—a tall, no-nonsense woman, the kind you wouldn't have wanted to mess with.

"Yes?"

I hadn't planned what to say.

"What do you want?" She was getting impatient.

"Just to see the place," I whispered.

"We don't take in guests, lady," she said, giving no sign of having recognized me. "This is not a *casa particular*."

"Bárbara, I'm Lorenzo's old girlfriend."

A look of shock passed over her face. She stared at me.

"Sorry," I mumbled, embarrassed. "I didn't want to impose. I came back to Havana and thought—"

Her expression softened.

"Ah, Merceditas! You look like a foreigner, girl. Come on in."

Bárbara moved away from the threshold she had been blocking with her body. I apologized again, but she answered with a laugh that didn't sound genuine. "It's okay, *mija*. You just caught me off guard."

We entered a room furnished with a red sofa sleeper and three rocking chairs. Lorenzo's living room was now a bedroom. I could see the first steps of the wooden stairs that led to his attic. The ceiling was now painted green. I'd thought I would be stepping into a minefield of memories, but the place looked like a stranger's home. Which it was. Bárbara and her family had ended up with the entire floor for themselves.

"It looks nice," I said when my snooping became obvious.

"Thank you. We've put a lot of work into it."

Someone moved upstairs. The attic floor creaked. My legs trembled like slices of flan.

Bárbara fingered her hair.

"Since Lorenzo didn't have family, me and the kids were allowed to move in when he . . . It was fair, seeing that we were four people crammed in together."

"Of course."

"Take a seat, *mija*."

The sofa was saggy and smelled of mayonnaise and oranges. There were crumbs of bread all over. I chose the less messy corner.

"Sorry my boys are such pigs. They're teenagers. Last time you saw them they were little, eh?"

"Yes."

Bárbara sat down too, fixed me with her astute eyes and didn't waste more time with small talk.

"What's up, Merceditas? Why are you here?"

"Like I said, I wanted to see—"

"Don't try to pull that on me! It's been almost ten years, and now you 'want to see' the place? *¡No jodas!*"

Her up-front attitude was oddly relieving. She slapped her thighs and let out another fake laugh.

"If there's treasure hidden inside one of these walls, we'll go halves!"

"No treasure, I'm afraid. But I'd like to ask you a couple questions."

She kept a blank expression. "Okay, go ahead."

"Was Lorenzo murdered?"

"What nonsense, Merceditas!"

I leaned over and whispered, "This is for my own peace of mind. I'm not going to tell the police or anybody else."

She said nothing, but I went ahead anyway. "Remember his Danish friend, the guy we used to call The Viking? Someone told me he had a fight with Lorenzo the night of the fire and killed him."

"That's right," said a clear voice.

Yulisa was standing at the bottom of the attic stairs. The studious, gawky preteen girl had turned into a stunning olive-skinned young woman with waist-long curly hair.

"*¡Niña, sio!*" Bárbara yelled. "Nobody was talking to you. Get out of here!"

Yulisa ignored her mother and addressed me, "I saw that guy sneak out of Lorenzo's apartment when the fire had just started."

She said his name with a pained, longing voice. She had had a real crush on him, and hadn't forgotten him either.

"Are you sure it was the Dane?"

"Totally. Big, tall and blond. Mom saw him too."

"Shut up!"

Bárbara leapt up from her seat, ready to slap her daughter. Yulisa didn't budge.

"Ladies, please calm down," I pleaded. "I didn't come here to cause trouble, just to find out the truth."

"You're not about to believe her, are you?" Bárbara huffed. "Yulisa was just a child then. This is a story she's made up as a result of reading too many of *his* stupid books."

Yulisa shook her head behind her mother's back. She hadn't been "just a child" then but almost a teenager, old enough to have a clear memory of the events.

"Several people visited Lorenzo after he returned from Villa Marista," Bárbara admitted. "The blond guy was one of them, yes, but he didn't come here that night."

"Who were the others?"

"How would I know? Colleagues of his, I guess. They looked like college types."

"But that evening, did you hear Lorenzo arguing with someone?" I insisted.

"No, he was alone all day. And for the record, I never heard Lorenzo argue with *anyone*. He was a considerate neighbor. Look, Merceditas"—she touched my arm in a soothing gesture—"if I thought someone had killed him, I would have told the cops. By the way, *we* were the main suspects until they found out that the fire had started in his side of the house."

"Were you here that evening?"

"We were all here. The kids had a new video game and were playing it."

Could the noises that Javier had heard come from the game? Not likely. But what else—?

"It broke my heart that Lorenzo died when he was still so young and full of life," Bárbara sniffled. "He might have thought no one cared for him."

The implicit accusation worked. Guilt gnawed at me.

"The police couldn't even find anyone willing to identify his body, so *I* had to do it." She exhaled heavily. "One of the worst days of my life, I swear."

"Did he look . . . bad?"

"Yes, *mija*. Very."

"Tell me, Bárbara, what do you think happened?"

"He committed suicide," she said matter-of-factly. "Just like his mother: poured kerosene over himself and lit a match."

"Why?"

"Don't you know his history, Merceditas? He had a hard life. Lost his parents early, then those problems at work. You left him. His time in prison. All that caught up with him and he snapped. I am still so, so sorry that this happened because he was a good guy."

My eyes swelled, but I managed not to cry. Yulisa talked about the books Lorenzo used to loan her. Bárbara recalled how he would clean not only his part of the common hall but theirs as well. Which was true, but she seemed to have forgotten how much he had resented it.

"We were like family." She coughed delicately. "He would have been happy that we got his apartment instead of it going to a stranger. Of course, we had to spend a pretty penny repairing it, and our own part as well. There was a lot of damage. I think the fire spread so fast because of those damn books!"

"I kept the few that didn't burn," Yulisa said. "The ones that were in the attic."

Bárbara shrugged and rolled her eyes at me.

"She's in college, you know. Reading novels, poetry and all that crap at the University of Havana."

Despite her dismissive words, I heard pride in her voice.

I smiled at Yulisa. "The Faculty of Arts and Letters?"

"Yes. Hispanic studies with a concentration in Cuban literature."

"Good for you, girl."

With peace achieved, the conversation stretched for over an hour. Yulisa went back to the attic. Once we were alone, Bárbara insisted that Lorenzo had been depressed. She had brought him rice and beans several times, but he wouldn't touch the food. People came over to see him, but he didn't always answer the door. And yes, there had been a programmed blackout that evening.

"That's why I didn't react immediately when I smelled kerosene. Lorenzo had an old oil lamp that stank to high heavens. I figured he was getting it ready for the blackout."

In the end, I pretended to accept her version. We said goodbye and even hugged each other. Yulisa came down and hugged me too, slipping a piece of paper into my hand. I palmed it and exchanged a knowing glance with her.

Bárbara escorted me to the hall. I went downstairs. Back in the little park, I sat again on "the loveseat" and read the note scribbled with a pencil on a notebook page: *The blond guy killed Lorenzo. We saw him walk out of the apartment. Mom made me swear not to tell anyone. I had to obey her then, but will tell the police now if you want me to.*

I let the paper fall down. So that was it. Javier was

right. The Viking had killed Lorenzo. They must have gotten into a fight. Over me? If so, was it my fault?

It had to be, I concluded. Everything had been my fault, from the beginning to the bitter end.

The tears I had been holding back spilled over. They were for Lorenzo and our life together that I had thrown away. For the woman I could have been with him. For my stupid encounter with Kiel. For my affair with Nolan.

I cried until my throat and eyes hurt and I was out of tears. Or so I thought, but no, there were still more left. I found myself weeping for my husband, Javier, even Selfa. We all had done wrong, but my offenses were worse because I had strayed from true love.

An ambulance raced down Trocadero Street, its siren piercing the crisp air. How long had I been there? I reached for my purse to look at my cellphone. Then I saw them: two gardenias lying next to me on the bench, still covered in dewdrops.

PART IV:
Letters from the Heart

1: From Mercedes

Most Coldwood Condos units didn't have dining rooms. Our kitchen doubled as a dining area but was too small, even for the little round table where Nolan and I ate. The matching chairs felt cheap and fragile after the antiquated but solid furniture at Villa Santa Marta. And the view was our next-door neighbor's unkept postage-stamp backyard.

A sofa that I hated was the living room's focus. Nolan had hauled it from his former house, the one he had shared with Lou Ellen and the kids. It was a big, ugly, boxy thing, canary yellow with blue stripes, stained and scratched. Though I had wanted for years to throw it in the nearest dumpster, he insisted on keeping the eyesore, whether out of sentimental reasons or so as not to spend on a better-quality piece.

But the minute I stepped in, fresh from Havana, the sight of the derelict sofa made me burst into tears. It reminded me of Nolan with his feet up, watching *Sixty*

Minutes or *The Rachel Maddow Show*, turning to me to comment or, more often, pontificate about current events. Suddenly alone in our shared home, I realized how much I missed him. Yes, contrary to what Candela and, at times, Nolan himself thought, I had *loved* him. Maybe not as much as I had loved Lorenzo, but we had been together longer. Nolan and I had had nine years to argue and get mad at each other, but had also developed a set of comforting routines, like me making Cuban-style coffee and milk for him in the mornings or telling him about my furry customers after he was done grading his students' work. Now he was gone.

Or was he? Had The Viking killed him too? Or was he hiding? But from whom?

In my mind I kept traveling back to my last days in Havana, asking myself if I could have done something different.

After recovering from the gardenia shock and hastily hiding the flowers in my purse, I fled the Trocadero Street park, hailed an *almendrón* on Paseo del Prado and went back to Villa Santa Marta. Mamina couldn't understand why I was sobbing, shaking and unable to speak.

"You'll find your Nolo," she repeated. "He couldn't have disappeared on you. Nobody harms tourists here."

Later that afternoon, I called the ship and explained that, since I hadn't found my husband yet, I was going to wait for him in Havana. The guy who answered the phone didn't seem sure how to react.

"Eh . . . I believe you need to come back with us. You can't stay in Cuba on your own."

"Says who? This is my country!"

My call was passed on to a higher-up.

"Do you think your husband is in danger?" he asked. "Any trouble?"

He sounded nervous.

"Not really," I lied. "He has friends here. He must be with them."

"Indeed! Enjoy your stay, Ms. Spivey. It's not uncommon for people to explore the city on their own during these short cruises."

He must have been relieved that they didn't have to report a second "accident" or another missing passenger. My call let them off the hook.

Afterward I walked to the Miramar police station and filed a *Denuncia de Desaparición Personal*. But I didn't mention the gardenias or the incidents on board the *Narwhal* because they sounded unbelievable and too much like a movie plot. It would be better, I reasoned, to keep it simple, so I just said that my husband hadn't returned to the ship after going to La Madriguera. I *did* mention Doctor Fernández, even if I was by then convinced that no such person existed.

A nice and very young lieutenant, who wasn't precisely "overzealous," told me that they needed to wait forty-eight hours to begin an investigation.

"He may just be lost, comrade."

He also suggested I call the American embassy. Which I did. They hadn't heard of Nolan. I asked Satiadeva to take me back to La Quinta de los Molinos and La Madriguera. Nobody had seen any American there.

"Have you tried Varadero Beach?" a Quinta de los Molinos employee asked, smirking. "Many tourists end up there. Drunk."

After all my efforts to locate Nolan failed, I hid at Villa Santa Marta until my Miami flight left.

ONCE IN GAINESVILLE, I immediately filed a Missing Person Report, hoping it would be taken more seriously than the *Denuncia*. I met with Detective Jess Dupre, a forty-something police officer, and, as I had done in Cuba, gave him an abbreviated version of the story. I focused on Nolan's disappearance, but left out Selfa, Javier and Kiel. Even if The Viking had killed them, and Lorenzo, I had no way to prove it.

It turned out that Detective Dupre knew about Nolan's dismissal.

"My son goes to Point South," he said. "Word got around, and students weren't happy to hear that the administration had canned Doctor Spivey. They all enjoyed his classes."

It was a small comfort. I wondered if Nolan had heard that.

"Was your husband depressed after he was let go?" Dupre asked.

"He took it hard at first, but later lined up several interviews at the upcoming Modern Language Association's convention," I answered. "He was confident he could get a new position and was looking forward to it."

"Did he act differently on the days prior to the trip? Did he have sleep problems? Moodiness?"

"Not that I could tell. I mean, he was very unhappy about the job situation, but other than that—"

"Did he ever talk about harming himself?"

"Goodness, no!"

When we got to our arrival in Havana, I just said that Nolan had gone to meet a Cuban professor and hadn't come back.

"Have you tried to contact that professor?"

"I don't know how. Nolan showed me an email the guy had written, but I don't remember the address."

"Do you know your husband's email password?"

"No. I never thought of asking him."

Dupre scratched his forehead.

"Sorry to ask this, Mrs. Spivey, but is there any possibility that he could be having an affair, meeting another woman or—? Did you notice anything suspicious in that department?"

My cheeks burned.

"The wife is always the last to know, right? But I don't think so. He isn't the kind—" I stopped mid-sentence. He *was* the kind. Or used to be. The detective gave me a thoughtful and somewhat sorry look.

"At this point, Mrs. Spivey, we'll be treating the case as voluntary disappearance, since there's no reason to suspect foul play. Let's start by contacting the American embassy in Havana and we'll go from there."

"But I already did!"

"That was a few days ago, wasn't it? Let's try again. I'll call you as soon as I hear from them."

There wasn't much I could say after that. Dupre's casual attitude made me want to mention Kiel, but I didn't even know how to spell his name. If I told him about my suspicions, he might laugh me out of the office. As it was, he seemed to regard me as a foolish, possibly cheated-on wife.

I wished he was right.

BACK AT HOME, I remembered the shadow I had seen in the backyard months ago. Just how easy it was for outsiders to enter Coldwood Condos? And now I was alone! The thought of having a burglar alarm installed started to creep up on me.

I stayed awake for hours every night. When I finally fell asleep, I saw Selfa drowning, her own nightmare turned into reality. The thump on Javier's skull and Nolan's cries for help in the darkness of La Quinta de los Molinos sounded loud and clear inside my head. One particularly horrible night, I dreamed that *I* had killed them. Sometimes during those desperate hours before dawn, I wished I was dead too.

The memory of the two gardenias haunted me. Who could have left them on the bench? Who knew about them?

Lorenzo, of course. But he wasn't about to come back from the dead to bring me flowers.

Nolan too. I had once mentioned the gardenias, which resulted in a stupid argument about my "former love life." But he had probably forgotten. That had been years ago.

Though it was possible that Lorenzo had said something to Kiel, I doubted it. Guys don't usually talk to other guys about flowers. And then, why would Kiel have left them quietly by my side instead of—I don't know, throwing them down my throat? That would have made more sense if he was in the business of avenging Lorenzo. But since he had killed him . . .

Then my mind's pendulum would swing. Nolan had been so shaken by the way Point South treated him that he could have decided to live in Cuba, since he seemed to believe it was a better and more egalitarian society. He would get in touch with me again after securing a position at the University of Havana. Maybe he hadn't been joking when he talked about it! Javier's death had been ruled an accident. I hadn't seen Kiel on the ship, so it was safe to assume he hadn't been there at all. And Selfa . . . well, she was probably home, taking care of her grandson.

As for the gardenias—couldn't they have been simply *flamboyán* flowers that happened to fall on the bench by my side? I had been so nervous, almost frantic, that such a mix-up wasn't impossible. There was no way to find out now because I had disposed of the flowers at Villa Santa Marta, before Mamina could see them.

Speaking of, I owed her a letter. A brief note would have to do, as I was in no mood for writing. I sat at the kitchen table with pen and paper and began:

Dear Mamina,

I'm back at home, missing you and still waiting for Nolan to show up. I am sure he's fine, though.

It was wrong to start with a lie, but the last thing she needed was to worry about me or my vanishing husband.

I'm sending this with a care package—

Of course, I had never recovered the one left on the *Narwhal.*

The shampoo, toys and treats for Nena are from my friend Candela. I'm working at her pet salon and keeping busy. Being by myself is hard, and I can understand how lonely you have felt all these years in Villa Santa Marta. When everything goes back

*to normal, I'll make arrangements to go back and
see you more often or, if you can manage, bring you
here for a month or two.*

*Give my regards to Satiadeva when you see him
again.*

Take care, dear Mamina.
Love,
Merceditas

SATIADEVA HAD DRIVEN ME to the airport two days
after the *Narwhal* left and promised to keep an eye on
Mamina. I had studied his face and gestures, listened
to the cadence of his voice and concluded that my
earlier suspicions were absurd. There were no miracle
surgeries. That was the stuff of B movies, not real life.

I put the note in an envelope. It joined the care
package that would soon fly to Havana, thanks to one
of the many semilegal travel and cargo companies that
had burgeoned in Miami.

LATER THAT DAY I was walking to the mail room, when
a woman who had never bothered to say hello before
went out of her way to run into me.

"How's your husband? Haven't seen him in a while."

"He's fine, thanks."

Nosy neighbors were just one of the many nuisances that came with living in the complex.

In our mailbox I found a condo association bill that almost gave me a heart attack when I opened it. Three hundred dollars! For what? Mowing the lawn and trimming a few hedges? The useless security fence? We paid all our utilities. We didn't even have a parking space for my car! *¡Carajo!* If Nolan didn't come back, no way I was going to stay in that overpriced, pretentious box of air.

But I did hope, against all odds and my gut instincts, that he would come back.

2: A Text from Lou Ellen

Two weeks had passed. I was still waiting for Dupre to get back to me. How did the saying go? No news is good news? But that wasn't always the case.

I no longer believed that everything had been "a series of eerie coincidences." Truth is, I never had. And now fear had a firm grip on me. I couldn't forget Javier's terrified expression when we were walking on the promenade deck. He had seen something, or thought of something, and it had scared him into staying on board. Which, by the way, hadn't helped him in the end. If The Viking had killed him, Selfa and Nolan, I might very well be the next one—or the last one. When I went out, I kept watching around. I never saw anything suspicious, but that offered little comfort. The others hadn't seen it coming either, had they?

I got into the habit of putting the dining table behind the door at night since I didn't have enough money to pay for a burglar alarm. Pretty and Pampered was now my only source of income, and, sadly, it didn't pay too well.

It was there, bathing an impertinent Yorkshire terrier that wouldn't stop wiggling, when a text came through.

CAN WE MEET SOMETIME TODAY? THX LE

Upon returning, I had given Lou Ellen the sanitized version ("Nolan disappeared in Havana") and asked if he had called her. Not because I believed he had, but because that would have been the most natural thing to do if I didn't know what I knew. Or what I thought I knew. Now she was texting me.

"Do you think he's contacted her?" I asked Candela, incredulous.

She shook her head.

"¡No, chica, no! Why would the comemierda call his ex? Stop worrying so much. He'll be back soon with his tail between his legs. And then I hope you make him pay dearly. What a rat!"

Candela had gotten the sanitized version as well.

She had offered to read the Tarot cards for me once more, but I politely refused. I didn't want her finding out the truth (whatever that was) through her woo-woo means. I wished I could have gotten it all off my chest, but there was so much in my own past I'd have had to disclose for the story to make sense. I didn't know how she would react. "If you don't keep your own secrets, how do you expect others to keep them for you?" Mamina used to say when she heard me babbling to my friends.

Lou Ellen and I had talked every now and then over the years, but never about anything of substance. Of substance to *me*, that is. Only about Katy and Kayden—where they were going to stay on certain weekends, how to schedule Christmas and spring breaks. I usually let Nolan handle the arrangements because he was their father, of course, but also because Lou Ellen's thick Arkansas accent made it difficult for me to understand her. My Cuban accent likely didn't make things easy on her end either.

When their divorce was finalized, I had assumed she hated me. Who could have blamed her? But she had always been nothing but polite, even friendly. It took me years to realize that it wasn't just good manners on her part, but the quiet awareness that she had been the winner in the end. Everybody, from their children to coworkers and casual acquaintances, sympathized with her and despised me. And she had kept the house.

Nolan refused to have it sold because it provided stability to the kids, he claimed. Though he had taken a pay cut when we moved to Gainesville, he'd helped her with mortgage payments.

Because he is . . . was . . . a good man.

I started to sniffle. I used to make fun of him for being a crybaby and had turned into one myself.

"Karma," I said aloud, "you're a real bitch, you know?"

Candela sighed but didn't argue with me.

I texted Lou Ellen. SIX-THIRTY?

YES. NEWBERRY RD. STARBUCKS?

I replied with a thumbs-up, then turned to Candela.

"She's in Gainesville," I said. "It's odd, don't you think, that she has come all the way from Miami to talk to me?"

"Maybe she's here for another reason and just wants to touch base."

"Maybe."

I HAD STARTED DRIVING Nolan's green Subaru because it was in better shape than my battered Ford Taurus. But it felt strange, and more than once I instinctively walked toward the passenger's door before remembering that nobody was going to drive me around. I was on my own, and the certainty hit me as I crossed the Starbucks parking lot.

Lou Ellen was sitting near the window, looking prettier and younger than I remembered.

"Oh, there you are!" She smiled and stood up.

We shook hands. Actually, she took mine in hers as if we were good friends. I noticed her manicured nails and highlighted hair. She was wearing a floral dress and a thin gold chain with a single pearl. Not too shabby—in truth, quite chic.

She had been sipping a Caramel Ribbon Frappuccino. I bought a double shot of espresso. And then we talked. About Nolan and what could be going on with him.

"I reported it, but the detective didn't take it seriously. And I'm getting so worried—I'll drop by the police station again."

"I wouldn't bother," she said. "That's why I wanted to talk to you."

I waited. She pursed her lips. "Have you thought that Nolan may be trying to reinvent himself once more?"

Was that "once more" an allusion to our history? I let it slide and answered, "Well, he might have needed some 'reinvention' after he was laid off. He certainly needed a new job."

"He was laid off?" Her eyes widened. "When? He never said a word to me or Kayden."

It was my turn to be surprised.

"He didn't tell you? That was back in May."

A frown creased her forehead and she muttered, "Nolan's always been good at keeping secrets."

"Secrets?" I shrugged. "It was probably his being too outspoken that got him in trouble at Point South."

She let out a bitter laugh.

"Honey, are you really that naïve?"

Honey *un carajo*. But I listened quietly as Lou Ellen told me that, when Nolan and I began our affair in Havana, she had no clue and was of course never "okay" with it, as he had claimed. She had found out, like everybody else, the day I went to FIU looking for him.

I'd always suspected he had lied about that. But hearing the truth so casually from her as she sipped on a Starbucks Frappuccino lent a surreal quality to the present and shone a darker light on the past.

"That summer, he let two weeks go without calling me and the children." She placed her glass on the table and dabbed her mouth with a napkin. (The two weeks *we* had spent at Varadero Beach and Cayo Largo.) "I believed at the time that he was having a midlife crisis. Like male menopause."

"Male menopause? I don't—"

"What I mean," she said softly, "is that he could be having another affair. Behind *your* back this time."

I couldn't bring myself to tell her that Detective Dupre had mentioned the same thing. Which was ridiculous, as far as I knew. I squared my shoulders and looked her in the eye.

"It's not possible, Lou Ellen. He was feeling too down for that."

She waved her hand dismissively. "A new love interest is a good way to lift the fog of depression. For men, at least. So don't panic yet. That's all I wanted to say since you sounded so concerned over the phone."

Driving back to Coldwood Condos, I began to question if *I* had known Nolan as well as I'd thought. What if Lou Ellen and Dupre were right? My idea of Nolan staying in Cuba wasn't that far-fetched after all. What if he had chosen to start a new life there, or somewhere else, *with* someone else? Looking back, he hadn't been in a romantic mood since his troubles started. Our sexual life had taken a nosedive. I'd chalked it up to stress, but—

I stopped at an ATM to get cash and a bank statement. There were eight hundred fifty dollars in our joint checking account and a little over two thousand in savings. It didn't seem like much, considering that Nolan was making fifty-eight thousand a year, but he could have withdrawn a big chunk before leaving or opened a different account. Managing our money had been Nolan's domain since day one. After all, it was mostly his.

I parked the Subaru in our designated spot (my Ford lived on the street), and walked to the condo. In the living room was a framed picture of Nolan and me in Cancun, and I glared at it. Tired and irritable, I took an Advil to fight off a splitting headache. It didn't work, but two glasses of wine did the trick.

3: A Call from Katy

The view from the living room window wasn't much better than the one from the kitchen: a parking lot and the brick-veneer wall that separated Coldwood Condos from Butler Estates, a similarly plain and non-descript cluster of residential units. A green dumpster. A skinny guy walking a fat dog.

Next to Nolan's Subaru was a red Mazda Miata with a California license plate and a bumper sticker that read I'D RATHER BE SURFING. *Me too*, I thought. Maybe not surfing, but away from Gainesville. The conversation with Lou Ellen the day before still bothered me like a rock in my shoe. Not that I believed her, but still. It was unsettling. And now throwing in the money issue . . . The combined balance in our savings and checking accounts wasn't enough to cover more than two months' expenses, I figured out after looking at the quickly compounding bills. It would be a good idea to ask Candela for more hours at Pretty and Pampered.

Or find another job, something full-time and more stable. As a cook, maybe, and eventually a chef. People liked my dishes. Nolan was always praising them. Oh, Nolan! I sobbed quietly.

It was 7 P.M. I was curled up on the yellow sofa, looking at the TV without watching it, when my phone rang. The call came from a 575 area code number.

"Hello?"

"Good evening, Mercy. This is Katy."

I had already recognized *la malcriada*'s high-pitched voice and made a noncommittal noise that could pass for a greeting.

"You haven't heard anything from my dad, have you?"

"Not yet."

"You know what Mom's been saying . . . that he ran away with another woman?" Her voice was ragged. "That's not true. Please, don't let that idea get in the way of the investigation and mislead the police."

"I don't believe it either. But what do *you* know?"

"Nothing. Except that Mom is wrong. Dad might have had an accident in Havana, been kidnapped, gotten sick . . . But he wouldn't have left you. He adores you. He would kill for you!"

Her words stirred something deep within me. I swallowed hard.

"Mom's come up with this story of the midlife crisis because . . . well, she's only human. It makes her feel better to think he's treated you the same way he did her."

Katy was sobbing. My resentment melted. If I had had a father, I would have felt the same. I wished I could offer her some comfort but it'd have been a lie.

"Don't worry," I said softly. "I'm not giving up on him."

"I also want to apologize for the way I've behaved toward you. I shouldn't have disinvited Dad—or you, supposing you wanted to attend my wedding."

An overwhelming sense of sadness washed over me.

"It's fine, Katy. I totally understand."

After a few more minutes, finally we hung up. I stared at the picture of Nolan and me in Cancun and began to sniffle. Yes, *la* Katy had been a pain in the neck during the entire course of our marriage, and it was about time she owned it. But honestly, she had had reasons to be pissed off at "the Cuban homewrecker." How many people would have been happier—including, perhaps, me—if I had stayed with Lorenzo in Cuba?

And she was right. Nolan did love me. Way more than I did him.

He would kill for you!
Would he?

ANOTHER DAY, ANOTHER TERRIER. Actually, one terrier and a dignified German shepherd who maintained great composure and didn't deign to bark at the yappy long-haired chihuahua that waited for his turn across from us. *If* I ended up living alone, it might be worthwhile to get a big, smart, well-mannered dog for company.

I was grateful for my Pretty and Pampered job but came back exhausted. I had been working by myself lately. Candela was in Miami taking an exam to become a certified dog trainer.

"Don't push yourself too hard," she told me before leaving. "I know how stressed you get. If you need to reschedule an appointment, please do so."

Of course I didn't. I had gone to three restaurants, nosing around about possible jobs, but there were none. One had asked for my résumé. It was embarrassing; I hadn't had any idea what to put on it.

When our checking account was depleted after paying several overdue bills, I had to go to the bank and transfer everything we had in savings. Nolan had done all that online, but I didn't even know the username or password. Which made me realize for the first time how dependent I had been on him. He had protected me—maybe overly so—and I had been living in a bubble for too long. Now it had burst, leaving me vulnerable and unequipped to function like an adult. It had been so easy, letting him do all the work and whining when things didn't go my way. A spoiled brat, no better than Katy. Well, if he happened to be somewhere, in Havana or Aruba or Paris, I would willingly take him back, no questions asked.

The investigation crawled along. Detective Dupre asked for Nolan's laptop. He kept it in his office for a few days, but returned it saying it held no clues. He had also requested a bank statement from both our accounts. The only transactions showing were the ones I had made. He checked Nolan's cellphone records. There had been no activity on his phone after two calls from a restricted number on the day we arrived in Havana. Doctor Fernández's? Dupre had contacted the Cuban police and was trying to track down the number but had gotten no response. They still seemed to think that there was no foul play.

I knew better.

CANDELA RETURNED, HAVING SUCCESSFULLY passed her examinations. But the business wasn't going all that well, now that a PetSmart had opened nearby and started taking away our clientele. She wanted to move to Miami and suggested we go together and share an apartment. But how could I? No matter how much I disliked the condo, it was still our home. Nolan's and mine. I couldn't just up and leave.

Seeing that there were no prospects of extra hours at the pet salon, I continued searching for jobs. In lieu of a résumé, I came up with a menu to present to potential employers. Some Cuban-style dishes, simple but full of flavor: slow-roasted, zesty suckling pig, yucca with garlic sauce, fluffy white rice and puréed black beans. For dessert, caramel flan and guava pastries. A festive fare, very much unlike my mood at the moment, but I "rehearsed" it several times. Unfortunately, I didn't get any callbacks from the restaurants where I'd offered my services. Candela and I ended up pigging out like crazy after each try.

4: From Mamina

Dear Merceditas,

How are you, mijita? *And that husband of yours, is he back? If he isn't, don't worry. He will return to you—if you still want him after all this trouble. You have more* sandunga *than any woman he can find, here or anywhere else!*

Mamina thought that Nolan was still in Cuba. So did Detective Dupre and Lou Ellen. Even I agreed with them—at times. But in my heart, I knew better. Katy kept calling. Her brother Kayden texted twice a week, asking if I had heard anything from or about his father. He didn't believe his mother's theory either. I answered the best I could but didn't dare give them any hope.

I sighed and went back to my grandma's wobbling handwriting.

You know who's been visiting me a lot lately? The almendrón *driver. I can't say his name for the life of me, so I call him Sato. He changed two lightbulbs in the dining room and fixed the shower in the upstairs bathroom. He also told me about a construction crew that can repair the living room. Not that I'm looking forward to having a bunch of strangers here, but . . .*

It was nice of Satiadeva to keep in touch. I hadn't expected him to and didn't really understand why, other than he was a good, caring guy who realized Mamina needed help. Maybe she reminded him of his own grandmother. In any case, I appreciated it.

. . . you can supervise everything when you come again. So many people are going back and forth now! They live five or six months here and the rest of the year abroad. I am getting old, mijita, *and it's difficult to be alone in this huge empty house.*

If she only knew! Until I found another job, there would be nothing left for traveling "back and forth."

I got your package. Nena is enjoying the treats and

*the chew toys. The shampoo makes her hair so shiny
that she looks like a show dog now. Give my thanks
to your friend Candela. She is an* angelita!

*The little gifts were fine too, but please don't
overspend on me.*

My sweet, selfless Mamina. I would continue to send
her a regular allowance, no matter what I had to go
without. I shook my head, shooing away my financial
troubles, but the next paragraph took my breath away.

*Now, the washer and dryer were too much! Hon-
estly, I'd rather have you visit than get these fancy
pieces of equipment. I'm sure you intended these as
a surprise gift, but they are a nuisance, Merceditas.
Now I'll have to bother Sato again to have these
two big machines installed and figure out how to
turn them on.*

"*¿Qué locura es esta?*" I said aloud.

Remember how much I enjoyed my telenovela,
Letters from the Heart? *The show is over, but
Catalina recorded all the episodes, and we're
watching them again.*

Take care, mijita. *Call me whenever you have a chance, and keep writing real letters. And remember, no more fancy-schmancy appliances for me!*

Hugs from your Mamina

I put the letter away and dialed Mamina's number, long-distance cost be damned. We talked briefly about Catalina and Nena, then I asked, trying to sound nonchalant, "What did you write about the washer and dryer?"

"Sorry if I came out as ungrateful, Merceditas. They work quite nicely and have made my life easier. But I don't want you to keep spending money on stuff when you could use it to buy a plane ticket."

"When did you get them?"

"Around two weeks ago. They delivered them, which was very convenient. Imagine if I had to go pick them up on my own!"

"Who were 'they'?"

"I don't know, *niña*. Two young guys. I imagine they work for the agency you send things through."

"Oh, yes."

"Sato installed them. Poor guy had to adapt the electrical outlets. You know that everything in this house is older than me."

Could Satiadeva have—?

"Did you pay him?"

"He didn't want to accept anything, but I made him a good meal of ground beef, beans and rice."

We talked a little longer and I got off the phone without mentioning that I had nothing to do with the "surprise gift." It had occurred to me that the appliances might have come from Satiadeva. If he wanted to keep it a secret, I would respect that. It was heartwarming to know that there were still people who did good deeds without expecting anything in return.

5: From Don Wilson, Esq.

After another long, stinky day at Pretty and Pampered, I was ready to take a shower and get rid of the wet-dog smell when I remembered that I hadn't passed by the mail room of the apartment complex in over a week. I wasn't looking forward to more bills. Electricity, Internet, condo association fees, rent—*el diablo colorao*. But I couldn't keep avoiding the mail forever. A check might even show up. What would Candela say? Think positive? Bah!

As expected, there were two more bills—water and gas—and an official-looking envelope.

I placed the bills on the kitchen counter. They joined Dish and Verizon, both past due. Then I opened the envelope, finding inside a typed letter, a two-page document, a business card and—yes, a check. To my name, and with so many digits that my head started to spin.

The letter read:

Dear Ms. Spivey,

My law firm represents the estate of Kjeld Aksel Østergaard. Mr. Østergaard named you as his sole heir in his last will and testament.

We are making a final distribution of the sum of nine hundred thousand dollars and seventy-five cents. A check payable to you for that amount is enclosed.

A copy of the inventory and final accounting for the above-referenced estate is also enclosed.

Taxes on distributions are your responsibility.

If you have any questions regarding the distribution or enclosures, please contact me.

> *Yours respectfully,*
> *Don Wilson, Esq.*

It took some time for all that to click in. Kjeld Aksel Østergaard? I had to read aloud that mouthful of a name to realize that it was The Viking's. But it still made no sense.

After our failed encounter, we'd stayed clear of each other. We never spoke about what happened, or rather didn't, in the bungalow, silently agreeing it had been a mistake. By some bizarre twist, had I been the only woman The Viking had ever had real feelings for? Could he have been on the *Narwhal* after all, following me?

I reread the letter carefully, noting all the legal terms I had skimmed over the first time. *Wait*, I thought. If I was Kiel's "sole heir" and this Wilson guy represented his estate, then The Viking was dead.

And what did "Esq." mean, anyway?

A bottle of Bacardí rum that Candela had brought from Miami sat on the counter. I poured myself a stiff drink. Thusly fortified, I used my cellphone to google "esquire," which turned out to be just a fancy title for lawyer. I also found out that a certain Don Wilson had a law firm in Chicago. The name and address matched the ones on the card.

I kept drinking until I passed out in front of the computer.

IT WAS WAY PAST noon when I woke up. Too late for Pretty and Pampered, but I wasn't planning to go in anyway.

A cup of strong La Llave coffee helped me fight the hangover. I resisted the urge to have a glass of wine (the rum bottle was empty) before calling the lawyer. I needed to be as lucid as possible during this conversation. As much as I wanted and needed the money, I wouldn't be cashing that check until I understood why I was getting it or who had sent it. For all I knew, it could be a trap.

Don Wilson's voice sounded deep and gravelly. He spoke calmly, as if delivering inheritances from dead people to astonished "sole heirs" was regular business for him.

"I understand this comes as a surprise, Ms. Spivey. My client anticipated you wouldn't be expecting it, but he went to great lengths to make sure that you got that sum."

"But I barely knew . . . your client," I replied. "If he's who I think he is."

"Mr. Østergaard was a Danish citizen by birth who lived in the United States all his adult life. I began representing him when he was a teenager and got a settlement after his parents' wrongful death. What you are inheriting is the remains of it."

Some "remains"!

"I met Mr. Østergaard in Cuba," I said, imitating the lawyer's pronunciation of The Viking's last name, "but we weren't close friends or anything."

"He seemed to know you well, though. He gave me precise instructions on how to locate you."

"We weren't in contact after I left my country, and that was a long time ago. Why would he want to leave anything to me?"

The "esquire" took a while to reply. He likely thought I was a *burra*, asking so many questions when such a substantial amount had fallen into my lap.

"A last-minute impulse, perhaps?" he suggested. "Mr. Østergaard was an eccentric character, in my opinion. I saw him in person just a few times, when he was young. Afterward, we only exchanged Christmas cards. He emailed me about two months ago, out of the blue, to make the arrangements for his last will and testament. He was very specific about contacting you by mail as soon as he passed away."

"And when was that?"

"Last week."

He contacted this guy two months ago and died . . . last week? Yes, that could have put him on the Narwhal.

"When we talked, he mentioned he was very sick," the lawyer added. "He was aware that he didn't have much time left."

I tried to remember how old Kiel, or Kjeld, was. A few years older than Lorenzo, it had seemed. But it was about time to stop my inquiries. I thanked the lawyer, hung up and stared at the check for several minutes, coming to terms with the uncertainty that had become a constant in my life.

TEN DAYS PASSED. NOTHING changed, but I couldn't very well sit and wait anymore. I deposited the check in a new bank account that was only in my name and notified Coldwood Condos I wouldn't be renewing my lease. Then I started looking for a new home in Miami. I had stopped working at Pretty and Pampered, but went there occasionally to lend Candela a hand. She thought I was living off Nolan's savings and approved of it.

"If he ran away with a lover, you should spend as much as you can before his new woman gets her dirty paws on the money," she said.

How much I wished I could tell her what was going on! I also thought of going back to Detective Dupre and explaining everything. Only . . . what *was* everything? Strange as it might sound, Kjeld could have named me his heir. He was an eccentric all right.

6: From Lorenzo

The minute I set foot in what became my new home, I fell in love with it. The open living and dining space had three stained-glass windows with geometric patterns that let in plenty of beautifully filtered light. They were modern, like the house itself, but had what Candela called "a vintage vibe." The master bedroom was on the first floor, and there were two smaller rooms and a terrace upstairs. The breakfast nook in the kitchen opened to a backyard, where four palm trees gave the feel of being in the countryside, though it was just a few minutes from downtown Miami. It was like a newer, smaller and happier version of Villa Santa Marta.

To the surprise of the realtor, who seemed worried about me not being prequalified, I made an offer on the spot. She was even more shocked when I paid in cash. I moved in as soon as the escrow was over. A smooth transaction, all in all. All the furniture was new (I took only what was absolutely necessary from the condo) and Candela helped me find some period pieces in the antique stores she knew.

Though I didn't have to worry about the cost of phone calls anymore, I sent Mamina a laptop and paid for her Internet service. She wasn't enthused, but we both needed to enter the twenty-first century. She finally promised to look into "that email thing."

Detective Dupre had kept in touch for three months, but Nolan's case was still treated as a "voluntary disappearance." The American embassy in Havana had reported no contact with him. As for Doctor Fernández, Dupre said they had searched the University of Havana directory but there were several Fernándezes there. Since I wasn't sure about the first name (Luis?), the search could take some time.

I wanted to come clean about the inheritance. Not only was it the right thing to do, but if they ever found out I had been gifted that much money, how could I justify *not* mentioning it? I had nothing to hide. They could talk to Don Wilson, Esq., and track down the connection between Nolan and Kjeld Østergaard, if there was any.

I just had to take the plunge, go back to the police station and spit out all I knew.

NOLAN'S LAPTOP WAS IN one of the upstairs rooms. I had decided to keep it, after Dupre returned it, in case Nolan ever came back. In the meantime, I could use it as well. Nobody ever wrote to me, but if Mamina and I were going to start emailing, I'd better make sure that my Gmail account worked. Or I could create another. Uf. While waiting for the computer to wake up from its prolonged slumber, I thought of Nolan and the last time he had used it, probably to correspond with "Doctor Fernández."

I clicked on the last Word document that had been opened. I didn't expect to uncover a big secret or anything, but Lou Ellen's and Dupre's suspicions were still rattling around in the back of my mind.

Dear Mr. Anthony,

It's with great interest that I am seeking to apply for a high school Spanish teaching position with your school district. My expertise in Latin American literature and ample experience . . .

A deep sadness enveloped me. Nolan had even been looking at high schools! My husband had been a good, decent, hardworking man whom I hadn't truly appreciated. With faults, yes, but I wasn't blameless myself. I wiped my tears and fought the desire to leave the room.

My own account was still up from the last time I'd logged on. I was going through a ton of spam, deleting messages without looking, when a sender's name caught my attention. I stopped. Bright lights flashed before my eyes as if the Perseid meteor shower had just burst in my head.

From: lorenzoalvear@gmail.com
To: mspivey@gmail.com
Subject: Dos gardenias para ti

Dear Merceditas,

These are my last gardenias for you. I hope they are received with as much emotion as those I left on our little "loveseat" in the park. Not like the way you treated the poor flowers I once tried, unsuccessfully, to give you at the Zapata Street bus stop.

Mercedes! I could have understood if you'd eventually fallen in love with a younger guy, or someone able to offer you the comforts you wanted and deserved. In my late thirties and living on a Cuban professor's salary, I wasn't such a catch. But weren't there enough men in Havana? Why did you have to sleep with one of my friends?

Why did you have to sleep with two *of my friends?*

You already know what happened to me. I went to prison because of Selfa's accusations, and Kjeld, who was in Cuba at that time, helped me get out. But losing you had hurt me more than being imprisoned and jobless. I had nightmares in which I murdered you and Nolan. I burned all your photos, all the notes you had written to me, wishing I could burn you. *Other times I could only cry and hope you were doing well.*

The day Kjeld visited me shortly after my release, I was despondent. He became furious and said you didn't deserve my tears. My response was that you would always be "the woman of my life."

"The woman of your life, my ass!" he yelled. "She's a whore! She slept with me, okay? Look at me.*"*

He went into detail about when and how it had happened. I remembered how you two had been avoiding each other the last few months we were together—something I had noticed without giving it more careful thought. Suddenly, it made sense.

You were a puta *all right. And all the anger I had been holding back, I took out on Kjeld. I started pummeling him.*

It was senseless and cruel. He was the only one who had stood by me in the end! But I lost it, and things went downhill fast. Though he defended himself, Kjeld was no match for my pent-up fury. I knocked him unconscious. He fell. I went on beating him until he stopped moving. Then I realized he'd stopped breathing too.

He was dead.

Upon realizing what I'd done, my first impulse was to call the police and turn myself in. I'd be sent to the firing squad, and that would be the end of my sorrows. But when I looked at the dead body of the man who had been my best friend, an image came to me.

Fire.

*I thought of my mother's last moments inside that very apartment. It was as if she, or Kjeld himself, was trying to tell me something. A book came to my mind as well—*The Count of Monte Cristo, *the scene where Edmond gets inside Abbé Faria's burial sack to escape from the Château d'If. I could fake my own death, make it seem as if I had* killed myself, and take Kjeld's place. If it went well, fine. If it didn't, what did I have to lose anyway?

I took off Kjeld's clothes and dressed him in mine. I put on his wig, his pants, shirt and coat, then poured a bottle of kerosene over him and threw a match on his face. I left when the flames started to spread over the furniture and my books—ah, my beloved books!

Bárbara and her daughter were coming out of their apartment, but didn't realize it was me when I passed quickly by their door. I later heard that Bárbara identified the body as mine and got my part of the house added to hers. Even if she suspected the truth, it was in her best interest not to stir the pot.

I had visited Kjeld in the Comodoro Hotel bungalow enough times to know the place and his routines. I arrived at night and didn't talk to anybody. His passport and the notebook where he wrote all his passwords and the important stuff that he was afraid to forget were there. The next morning, I booked a flight to Mexico using his credit card. My disguise must have worked well enough because no one stopped me at the hotel or the airports.

What an ironic turn of fate. Of all my friends,

I was the one who'd never wanted to leave Cuba. I didn't understand their urgency to pull up their roots and travel far away. And there I was, a criminal fleeing to another country, when all I'd ever wanted was to teach at the Faculty, have my books published and grow old in a city I loved with the woman I loved . . .

Kjeld's affairs, which he had once told me about, were quite simple. Basically, he had an account with Chase Manhattan Bank where the settlement money had been deposited and he'd made some secure investments over the years. There was a lawyer, Don Wilson, who had been his legal guardian after his parents died, and I kept the contact.

After getting hold of the account, I considered looking for you. I was richer than Nolan. If money was all you wanted, you would come back to me. But the thought that you had betrayed me with two different men—that I knew of—held me back. I both loved and despised you.

My life wasn't bad for several years. Like Kjeld had, I read and traveled. But I never forgave myself for having killed him. And I certainly didn't want to harm anyone else. Even when my book came out and hit the bestseller list in Spain, I felt no desire to expose Javier. Yes, everyone had betrayed me, but I would take the high road. Let them have it. After all, Lorenzo Alvear was dead and forgotten. I was now Kjeld Østergaard.

I settled in San José del Cabo, a small Mexican town near Cabo San Lucas. I kept to myself, wrote three more books and had them published under a nom de plume, but they never reached the success of Las Perseidas, *or whatever Javier retitled it.*

In 2013 I got sick. My weakest organs, my kidneys, failed me like they had failed my mother before me. It might have happened anyway—I'd inherited bad genes—but I can't help thinking that I would have lived longer had you stayed with me.

I bought a new kidney. My body rejected it. The other began to shut down too. I went on dialysis, but more complications arose: my teeth fell out, my vision blurred, I had trouble retaining food. I had an expiration date. Knowing that, I did what I had avoided all those years.

I looked for each of you.

Javier was in Madrid, writing for travel magazines and still getting royalties for my book. Selfa headed the Literature Department at the Faculty of Arts and Letters. Nolan and you had moved to Gainesville, where he was a college professor. Everybody was doing quite well, it seemed. Better than they deserved.

As my health deteriorated, the old rage returned with a vengeance. Embittered and sick, I came up with a revenge plot and set the plan in motion two years ago. Fortunately, there was still enough left in Kjeld's account.

But hired hands are sloppy. Javier didn't die in the "accident" he had in Madrid, though the resulting injury was bad enough to end his travel-writing career. They did better with Selfa's son in Miami. It would have been riskier to target her in Cuba. Besides, I knew her son's death would hurt her more than anything else.

Ay, Merceditas. I didn't know I had so much evil in me.

Selfa moved to Miami to take care of her grandkid. That was even better for my purposes because I wasn't done with her.

There was still Nolan to be dealt with. And you.

I started to correspond with him, pretending to be a Faculty of Arts and Letters professor. The problem was that the Faculty had never paid for a foreigner's visit, and I didn't want him to get suspicious by offering to buy his plane ticket. The "free cruise" for you, him and Selfa fixed that. As for Javier, Casa de las Américas, an organization he had been courting since we met in Havana, was the perfect come-on.

In the meantime, I often passed by the pet salon. You still looked pretty but not as happy and care-free as I remembered—of course, that might have been wishful thinking on my part. I circled the condo and once dared to look through your kitchen window. You must have sensed it, or heard something, because you went outside and started poking around. That was a close call.

Going on the cruise with all of you was a bit risky too. But by then I had lost so much weight that no one could have recognized me. Still, to be on the safe side, I boarded the Narwhal *wearing a wig, like Kjeld used to, and a fake beard and a hat.*

Finally, we all were on the same boat.

Selfa was the first to go. She wandered by herself into a deserted area of the ship where the lifeboats were stowed. I got behind her, pretending to take pictures, hit her in the head with my camera and threw her overboard. She cried for help, but nobody heard her. She never knew it was me. Not exactly what I had envisioned, but the chance was too good to be missed. It all happened so fast that I didn't have time to enjoy it—if there was anything to be enjoyed. She was there one second, and then she wasn't. I came out sort of empty, but told myself that "the next one" would be better.

Then you and Javier met. The possibility had worried me, but I had no way to prevent it. When I came around and eavesdropped on your conversations, it was clear you suspected something. Hopefully, not the truth, I thought. You and I were never face-to-face on board, though we came close once or twice.

With Javier, it was a different story. We did come face-to-face the second day, on the promenade deck. He got so pale and shocked that I feared he had recognized me. But he kept quiet. Maybe he didn't believe his own eyes. Or that might have been the reason why he stayed on board.

I figured that you and Nolan would split up in Havana—no way you would have gone to a lecture about Manuel Cofiño! When you left in the almendrón, *I waited in Cathedral Square and followed him to La Madriguera in a rental car. I texted him that the lecture had been canceled and suggested we meet at the nearby Quinta de los Molinos to schedule a new one. He was a little wary, but ended up falling for it.*

My original plan was to let him know who I was before it was over. But I didn't dare to. He could have cried for help, and there were many people outside La Quinta and in La Madriguera. I relied on the surprise factor again, and it worked well. So did a machete I had bought in a tourist trap on Empedrado Street. Quite a sharp blade it had. In case you care to find it, Nolan's body is rotting in a pond behind the Máximo Gómez Museum.

Oddly, just like it had happened with Selfa, I got no satisfaction when the bloody remains of "Doctor Spivey" sank in the mud. I kept thinking he deserved it, but couldn't quite convince myself.

I returned to the ship, expecting you would be there. You weren't. By then waves of remorse and grief were sweeping over me. My Monte Cristo-esque revenge plot, which had made me so proud at first, looked pointless now. Evil. Dangerous too. I could end up spending my last few days in a Cuban jail after all.

Javier had also messed up my plan by staying

on board, but I was now glad for it. He was just a poor devil whose real books no one liked. And he had believed I was dead when he stole mine.

In the evening, the Narwhal left the bay for the meteor shower watch. That was the only true coincidence in the whole thing. I hadn't even thought of Las Perseidas when I decided to have everyone gathered on a cruise ship in August.

Around midnight, disheartened and unable to sleep, I wandered into the library. Javier was there. He yelped when he saw me. This time there was no doubt that he knew who I was. He tried to call onboard security and, at that point, I had no choice. The bronze bust of Alexandre Dumas sitting nearby took care of him.

Despite myself, my plan had mostly succeeded. It was time to stop the madness. I wasn't a character in a nineteenth-century French novel, but a flesh and blood man who had committed a series of dreadful acts. But I still wanted to see you again, and had started to suspect you wouldn't be back to the ship. Maybe you, like Javier, had realized I was alive.

The next morning, I drove the rental car to your grandmother's house. (Where else could you have been? I had totally forgotten about Mamina.) I saw *her washing clothes by hand in the backyard. At her age, Merceditas! I thought that you, at least, cared for her.*

I tailed the almendrón *all the way to the terminal building, then walked behind you to Trocadero Street. You went upstairs. To talk to Bárbara and her kids? To look at my old place? I waited in the park until you came back, collapsed on the bench and started crying your eyes out. Were you crying for me?*

I almost stepped out of the shadows to comfort you. If you had stayed there longer, I might have, and perhaps everything would be different now—or not. It was too late for me anyway.

I left Havana, feeling, for the first time, at peace.

Back home—if I can call it home—I contacted the lawyer who had once managed Kjeld's affairs and arranged for him to give you what is left of his money.

I'll program my Gmail account to send this message when I am closer to the end. Even if you don't get it, you're smart enough to figure everything on your own. You aren't a burra, *though I know I used to call you that jokingly.*

Have a good life, Merceditas. I know I've done many wrongs, but I hope you'll think kindly of me, at least once a year, when the Perseids come back.

Yours,
Lorenzo

I sobbed for hours, alternatingly hating Lorenzo and mourning him. With a biting awareness, I realized that a part of me had suspected he was still alive—the part that kept trying to find likeness of him in Satiadeva and others, and went back to the apartment looking for him. The part that, despite everything, had never stopped loving him.

7: Like a Novel

The white office walls were lined with shelves full of books, folders and a couple of pictures, one of them of Detective Dupre and a young man on the Point South College sprawling campus. Dupre had listened to my long and rambling account with patience and, it seemed at times, slight disbelief.

"Your life," he said at last, "sounds like a novel. You should write a book about all that."

"There're already too many writers in the world, and they tend to cause trouble," I said. "Plus, who's going to read a book written by *me*?"

"You never know, do you?"

After recovering from the shock, I had printed Lorenzo's email and taken it to the Gainesville police station, where I had shown it to Dupre and told him everything. Yes, *everything*. Not the abbreviated and sanitized version, but the whole story, starting with my meeting Lorenzo in college, cheating on him with

Kjeld, leaving him for Nolan, what happened with *Las Perseidas* and so on and so forth. The pure and simple truth, which was, of course, sticky and complicated. I also shed more tears, which might have helped convince him I was telling the truth.

We were talking for over three hours, with Dupre interrupting me every so often to clarify some points.

"Before you went on that cruise, did you ever suspect that your ex-boyfriend wasn't dead? Did you try to warn your husband after realizing he was in danger?"

I answered no and yes. It wasn't until the "coincidences" started to pile up aboard the *Narwhal* that I realized something was amiss. But the idea of Lorenzo being alive had never been a conscious thought, just the ghost of a hope—or dread. And I had warned Nolan, more than once. I was drunk, but he could have stayed away from that damn Quinta de los Molinos as I'd pleaded with him to do. I *had* tried.

NOW DUPRE AND HIS team can move ahead with the investigation. Marlene Martínez—Candela's cousin—contacted her former National Revolutionary Police colleagues, who agreed to cooperate with the Gainesville Police Department. They will drain the La Quinta de los Molinos ponds until they find Nolan's body.

Not just to confirm my story, but to bring closure for his kids.

There are some things I'll never know, like why Bárbara hadn't let Yulisa tell the cops about Kjeld. So as not to stir the pot, like Lorenzo thought? Or because she had recognized him, realized what he had done and wanted to protect him? Another mystery is why The Viking claimed to have slept with me, when it technically hadn't happened. Maybe he'd just wanted to convince Lorenzo I wasn't worth his pain. And lastly, what punishment had Lorenzo planned for me, had I been on board when he thought I'd be? Funny how he left *that* part out of the letter. But honestly, I don't think he would have ever harmed me.

It doesn't matter now. Like Javier once said, *lo pasado, pisado*.

I talked to Lou Ellen, though sparing her the unnecessary, gruesome details. She was upset, but not *too* sad. It was much harder for the children, of course.

At first I was afraid that the courts, the police or some powers that be would order me to return the money, seeing that it hadn't come from the real Kjeld. But he didn't have any family, at least in the United States. In any case, I spent half of it fast on my new house. I also opened an account for Mamina in the

Royal Bank of Canada and, since Nolan had no life insurance policy, I gave Lou Ellen two hundred thousand dollars for Kayden's college fund.

Out of generosity? Guilt? Who knew? The past was over, but I wanted to start my new life with a clean conscience. Kjeld's inheritance was, in more than one way, blood money. And despite what Lorenzo thought of me, money wasn't all I wanted. I'd loved Nolan. I'd loved Lorenzo too. My heart was a four-hundred-page book like the ones he liked to read.

Speaking of, I just ordered a copy of *Light in Transit*. I also borrowed *The Count of Monte Cristo* from the local library. Why didn't it surprise me that the protagonist's love interest was named Mercedes too?

AFTER I HAD A house paid for, and enough to repair Mamina's, I wanted to become self-supporting. I would never again be in the desperate position I'd found myself when my only job was a part-time gig at Pretty and Pampered. *No, señor.* Marlene and I discussed the addition of a cafeteria with a Cuban-style menu to La Bakería Cubana. Her clients were asking for it, she said, but she was more of a baker than a cook. I'd made *arroz con pollo imperial* when she had once visited with Candela, and she had been impressed.

"You're a natural chef," she said.

The bakery's tempting smells of burned sugar, cinnamon and freshly made bread started calling me. When I went there for flan or éclairs, I found excuses to get in the kitchen. I'd always admired the way Marlene had "reinvented" herself and become an entrepreneur. I could do something similar. Something productive with my life, you know? I might not be college material, but there's a lot you can achieve with two hands and a desire to get ahead.

Marlene could also help me to track down my mother, or at least find out what had happened to her. We talked about it over virgin piña coladas. I'd decided to steer clear of alcohol for good. If I hadn't been so *borracha* when I tried to warn Nolan, maybe . . .

IT WAS EARLY DECEMBER when Marlene and I met again at the bakery because I'd agreed to help her plan a Christmas dinner for Candela and a few other friends. *Navidad* was around the corner and I didn't want to spend it alone.

The menu was the same I had prepared during my darkest hours, when I was terrified and running out of money. Some Cuban-style dishes, simple but full of flavor: slow-roasted, zesty suckling pig, yucca with garlic sauce, fluffy white rice and puréed black beans. For dessert, caramel flan and guava pastries. Festive fare, very much like my current mood.

Candela, who had also moved to Miami to open a second Pretty and Pampered, gave me a hard time for not having trusted her from the beginning.

"*Coño, chica*, I thought that we were friends. How could you have kept all those secrets to yourself? What am I, *la pata de un puerco*?"

Nosy as she is, Candela was full of questions about Lorenzo and his tale of revenge.

"I don't get it," she said. "How come nobody found out? Wouldn't his autopsy show discrepancies? What about dental records?"

"*Mija*, in Cuba the police use these sophisticated procedures only for high-profile cases, not a man who didn't even have a known relative to identify his body. The sad truth was that, like he said, nobody cared."

"And your grandma, what does she say about all that?"

"I didn't tell her everything."

My house and its old-fashioned furniture had also piqued Candela's amateur-collector's interest.

"You should have taken more pics, Merceditas. Is

it really Art Deco? I think the piano is a Steinway, right?"

"Why don't you come and see for yourself? You can stay with us."

"Your grandma won't mind?"

"No! She thinks that you're an *angelita*."

"*¡Vamos!*"

After that, she couldn't wait to meet Mamina—and Satiadeva.

"There are metaphysical groups there? Oh, I have tons of books and materials they can use, *chica*! I'll bring them all."

The two of us in Havana! I wasn't sure how that would turn out, or when it would happen, but you could bet we wouldn't be taking a cruise this time around.

ACKNOWLEDGMENTS

This book owes a great deal to many people. First, a big heartfelt thanks to my editors Juliet Grames, Amara Hoshijo and Yezanira Venecia for their suggestions, constant support and encouragement to put this novel and the Havana Mystery series into the world.

The first version of *Death under the Perseids* was written fairly quickly, in around three months. Every Thursday I would email twenty pages to Raquel Troyce, and we would discuss the plot over the weekend. And when I didn't send "mis veinte," she made sure to remind me. Then Ileana Pelaez went through the whole manuscript and sent me detailed notes that made the story clearer and stronger. Gracias, amigas.

And many, many thanks to my readers, por supuesto!